Goosebumps

Monster Blood II

He reached in and pulled out the plastic can.

He read the faded label: MONSTER BLOOD.

Then he read the words in tiny type below it: SURPRISING MIRACLE SUBSTANCE.

"I saved it," Andy said, beaming proudly.

Evan couldn't get over the shock. "You brought Monster Blood! I don't believe it! You brought Monster Blood!"

"No." She shook her head. "It's empty, Evan. The can is empty."

His face fell. He sighed in total disappointment.

"But you can show the can to everyone," Andy insisted. "That will prove you didn't make it up. It will prove that Monster Blood really exists."

Evan sighed again. "What good is an empty can?" he groaned.

He pulled off the top, peered inside—and screamed.

D1386012

Goosebumps

Monster Blood II

R.L. Stine

Hippo

Scholastic Children's Books,
Scholastic Publications Ltd,
7-9 Pratt Street, London NW1 0AE

Scholastic Inc.,
555 Broadway, New York, NY 10012-3999, USA

Scholastic Canada Ltd,
123 Newkirk Road, Richmond Hill,
Ontario, Canada L4C 3G5

Ashton Scholastic Pty Ltd,
PO Box 579, Gosford, New South Wales,
Australia

Ashton Scholastic Ltd,
Private Bag 92801, Penrose, Auckland,
New Zealand

First published in the USA by Scholastic Inc., 1994
First published in the UK by Scholastic Publications Ltd, 1995

Text copyright © 1994 by Parachute Press

ISBN 0 590 55862 5

Typeset by Contour Typesetters, Southall, London
Printed by Cox & Wyman Ltd., Reading, Berks

20 19 18 17 16 15 14 13 12 11

Evan Ross backed into the corner of the den as he stared at his dog Trigger.

The tan cocker spaniel lowered his head and stared back at Evan with wet, brown eyes. The old dog's tail began to wag excitedly.

"Trigger—" Evan cried angrily. "Have you eaten Monster Blood again?"

The dog's tail began wagging faster. Trigger let out a low bark that rumbled like thunder.

Evan's back pressed against the dark-panelled den wall.

Trigger took a few heavy steps towards him, panting hard. His huge pink tongue, as big as a salami, hung out of his enormous mouth.

"Have you?" Evan demanded. "Have you eaten more Monster Blood?"

The answer to Evan's question was obvious.

Trigger had been normal cocker spaniel size that morning. Now the dog stared down at Evan, as big as a pony.

Trigger's furry paws, the size of elephant feet, thudded on the den carpet. His enormous tail pounded louder than a bass drum against the side of a leather couch.

Evan covered his ears as Trigger let out an excited, high-pitched bark that shook the den walls. "Stay! Stay!" Evan shouted.

The enormous dog panted hard, his tail wagging furiously.

Oh, no! Evan thought in horror. He wants to play!

"Sit!" Evan screamed. "Sit!"

But Trigger didn't know how to sit. For ten years—*seventy dog years!*—Evan had tried to teach Trigger to sit on command.

But Trigger just didn't get it.

"Where did you find the Monster Blood?" Evan demanded. "We all saw it disappear into thin air. Gone. It was just gone. You know that stuff makes you grow. And grow and grow and grow. Where did you find it?"

Trigger tilted his big head at an angle, as if trying to understand Evan's words. Then, wagging his huge tail excitedly, he started to run to Evan.

No! Evan thought. He's going to jump on me! He's going to jump! If he jumps, he'll *crush* me!

An enormous glob of drool escaped Trigger's open mouth and hit the carpet with a loud *smack*.

"Sit!" Evan cried, his voice choked with panic. "Sit, boy! Sit!"

Trigger hesitated, staring down at Evan. To Evan's horror, the dog was growing even bigger. Trigger was now as tall as a horse!

Where did he find the container of Monster Blood? Evan wondered, his back pressed against the wall. Where?

The dog's brown eyes gaped at Evan like shimmering, dark pools. Trigger uttered another deafening bark that shook the whole house.

"Yuck!" Evan cried, squeezing his nose with two fingers. The dog's breath rushed at him like a strong wind. And it smelled as sour as a dead mouse.

"Back! Get back, Trigger!" Evan pleaded.

But Trigger had never learned that command, either.

Without warning, the giant dog leaped at Evan.

"Down! Down!" Evan shrieked.

Trigger's mouth gaped open. The dog's huge tongue licked the side of Evan's face. The tongue felt scratchy and hot. Evan's carrot-coloured hair was matted with sticky dog saliva.

"No—please!" Evan screamed. "I'm only twelve! I'm too young to die!"

He started to scream again. But Trigger's big teeth clamped around his waist, cutting off his breath.

3

"Trigger—put me down! Put me down!" Evan choked out.

The dog's wagging tail sent a lamp crashing to the floor.

The teeth held Evan gently but firmly. He felt himself being lifted off the floor.

"Put me down! Put me down!"

Why wouldn't the stupid dog listen?

Evan thrashed his arms and legs frantically, trying to squirm free. But Trigger held on tightly.

The dog's enormous paws pounded on the carpet. He carried Evan through the hall and across the kitchen. Then he lowered his head and butted the kitchen screen door open.

The door slammed hard behind them. Trigger began trotting over the grass.

"Bad dog! Bad dog!" Evan cried. His voice came out in a tiny squeak.

Had Trigger grown even bigger?

Evan was at least a metre off the ground now!

"Put me down! Down!" he cried.

Evan watched the green grass of the back garden bounce beneath him. Trigger was panting as he walked. The panting sounds made Evan's whole body vibrate. He realized his jeans and T-shirt were soaked from dog saliva.

Trigger doesn't mean to hurt me, Evan told

himself. He's just being playful. Thank goodness he's such an old dog. His teeth aren't very sharp.

The dog stopped at the edge of the flower bed at the bottom of the garden. He lowered Evan nearly to the ground, but didn't let go.

His paws began to churn up the soft dirt.

"Let me down!" Evan shrieked. "Trigger—listen to me!"

Breathing hard, his hot, sour breath pouring over Evan, the big dog continued to dig.

A wave of horror swept over Evan as he realized what Trigger was doing. "No!" Evan shrieked. "Don't bury me, Trigger!"

The dog dug faster, its front paws churning furiously. The soft dirt flew past Evan's face.

"I'm not a bone!" Evan cried frantically. "Trigger—I'm not a bone! Don't bury me, Trigger! Please—don't bury me!"

"Don't bury me. *Please* don't bury me!" Evan murmured.

He heard laughter.

He raised his head and glanced around—and realized that he wasn't home in his back garden. He was sitting in his assigned seat in the third row near the window in Mr Murphy's science class.

And Mr Murphy was standing right at Evan's side, his enormous, round body blocking the sunlight from the window. "Earth calling Evan! Earth calling Evan!" Mr Murphy called, cupping his chubby pink hands over his mouth to make a megaphone.

The kids all laughed.

Evan could feel his face growing hot. "S-sorry," he stammered.

"You seem to have been somewhere in Day-dream Land," Mr Murphy said, his tiny black eyes twinkling merrily.

"Yes," Evan replied solemnly. "I was dreaming about Monster Blood. I—I can't stop thinking about it."

Ever since his frightening adventure that summer with the green, sticky stuff, Evan had been dreaming and daydreaming about it.

"Evan, please," Mr Murphy said softly. He shook his round, pink head and made a "tsk-tsk" sound.

"Monster Blood is real!" Evan blurted out angrily.

The kids laughed again.

Mr Murphy's expression grew stern. His tiny eyes locked on to Evan's. "Evan, I am a science teacher. You don't expect a science teacher to believe that you found a can of sticky green gunk in a toy shop that makes things grow and grow."

"Y-yes, I do," Evan insisted.

"Maybe a science-*fiction* teacher would believe it," Mr Murphy replied, grinning at his own joke. "Not a *science* teacher."

"Well, you're stupid!" Evan cried.

He didn't mean to say it. He knew immediately that he had just made a major mistake.

He heard gasps all around the big classroom.

Mr Murphy's pink face darkened until it looked like a red balloon. But he didn't lose his temper. He clasped his chubby hands over the big stomach of his green sportshirt, and Evan could see him silently counting to ten.

7

"Evan, you're a new student here, isn't that right?" he asked finally. His face slowly returned to its normal pink colour.

"Yes," Evan replied, his voice just above a whisper. "My family just moved to Atlanta this autumn."

"Well, perhaps you're not familiar with the way things work here. Perhaps at your old school the teachers liked it when you called them stupid. Perhaps you called your teachers ugly names all day long. Perhaps—"

"No, sir," Evan interrupted, lowering his head. "It just slipped out."

Laughter rang through the classroom. Mr Murphy glared sternly at Evan, his face twisted in an angry frown.

Give me a break, Evan thought unhappily. Glancing quickly around the room, Evan saw a sea of grinning faces.

I think I'm in trouble again, Evan thought glumly. Why can't I keep my big mouth shut?

Mr Murphy glanced up at the wall clock. "School is nearly over," he said. "Why don't you do us all a little favour, Evan, to make up for the time you made us waste today?"

Uh oh, Evan thought darkly. Here it comes.

"When the bell rings, go and put your books away in your locker," Mr Murphy instructed. "Then come back here and clean Cuddles' cage."

Evan groaned.

His eyes darted to the hamster cage against the wall. Cuddles was scratching around in the wood shavings on the cage floor.

Not the hamster! Evan thought unhappily.

Evan hated Cuddles. And Mr Murphy knew it. This was the third time Mr Murphy had made Evan stay after school and clean out the smelly, disgusting cage.

"Perhaps while you clean the hamster cage," Mr Murphy said, returning to his desk, "you can think about how to do better in science, Evan."

Evan jumped to his feet. "I won't do it!" he cried.

He heard shocked gasps all around him.

"I hate Cuddles!" Evan screamed. "I *hate* that stupid, fat hamster!"

As everyone stared in amazed horror, Evan ran over to the cage, pulled open the door, and grabbed Cuddles up in one hand.

Then, with an easy, graceful motion, he flung the hamster across the room—and out of the open window.

Evan knew he was having another daydream.

He didn't jump up screaming and throw the hamster out of the window.

He only thought about it. *Everyone* thinks about doing crazy, wild things once in a while.

But Evan would never do anything that crazy.

Instead, he said, "Okay, Mr Murphy." Then he sat quietly in his seat, staring out of the window at the puffy white clouds in the bright blue sky.

He could see his own reflection staring back at him in the glass. His curly, carrot-coloured hair looked darker in the reflection. So did the freckles that dotted his cheeks.

His expression was mournful. He hated being made fun of in front of the entire class.

Why am I always getting myself into trouble? he wondered. Why can't Mr Murphy ever give me a break? Didn't the teacher realize how hard it was to be the new kid in school? How am I supposed to make new friends if Murphy is always making me look like a total jerk in class?

Bad enough that no one believed him about the Monster Blood.

Evan had eagerly told the kids in his new school about it. How he had stayed with his great-aunt the past summer. How he and a girl he met named Andy had found the blue container of Monster Blood in a creepy old toy shop.

And how the green, yucky Monster Blood had started to grow and grow. How it had bubbled out of its container, outgrown a bucket, outgrown a *bath tub*! And just kept growing and growing as if it were alive!

And Evan had told kids how Trigger had eaten just a little of the Monster Blood—and had grown nearly as big as a house!

It was such a frightening, amazing story. Evan was sure his new friends would find it really cool.

But, instead, they just thought he was weird.

No one believed him. They laughed at him and told him he had a sick imagination.

Evan became known around his new school as the kid who made up stupid stories.

If only I could prove to them that the story is true, Evan often thought sadly. If only I could show them the Monster Blood.

But the mysterious green gunk had vanished

from sight before Evan left his great-aunt's house. Not a trace of it had been left. Not a trace.

The bell rang. Everyone jumped up and headed for the door, talking and laughing.

Evan knew that a lot of his classmates were laughing at *him*. Ignoring them, Evan picked up his backpack and started to the door.

"Hurry back, Evan," Mr Murphy called from behind his desk. "Cuddles is waiting!"

Evan growled under his breath and stepped out into the crowded corridor. If Murphy loves that stupid hamster so much, why doesn't *he* ever clean out the cage? he wondered bitterly.

A group of kids laughed loudly as Evan passed by. Were they laughing at him? Evan couldn't tell.

He started jogging to his locker—when something hit his leg just above the ankle. His feet flew out from under him, and he toppled face down on to the hard tile floor.

"Hey—!" Evan cried angrily.

He stared up at a big, tough-looking kid from his class named Conan Barber. All the kids called him Conan the Barbarian. For good reason.

Conan was twelve, but he looked about twenty years older! He was taller and wider and stronger and nastier than any kid in the school.

He wasn't a bad-looking guy, Evan grudgingly admitted. He had wavy, blond hair, blue eyes, and a handsome face. He was very athletic-looking, and played all the sports at school.

He was an okay guy, Evan thought wistfully. Except that he had one very bad habit. Conan loved to live up to his nickname.

He *loved* being Conan the Barbarian.

He loved strutting around, pounding kids who weren't his size—which included *everyone*!

Evan had not hit it off with Conan.

He met Conan in the playground a few weeks after moving to Atlanta. Eager to make a good impression, Evan told him the whole Monster Blood story.

Conan didn't like the story. He stared back at Evan with his cold, blue eyes for a long, long time. Then his expression hardened, and he murmured through clenched teeth: "We don't like wise guys down here in Atlanta."

He gave Evan a pretty good pounding that day.

Evan had tried to stay away from Conan ever since. But it wasn't easy.

Now he gazed up at Conan from his position on the floor. "Hey—why'd you trip me?" Evan demanded shrilly.

Conan grinned down at him and shrugged. "It was an accident."

Evan tried to decide whether it was safer to stand up or to stay down on the floor. If I stand up, he'll punch me, he thought. If I stay down here, he'll step on me.

Tough choice.

He didn't get to make it. Conan reached down and, with one hand, pulled Evan to his feet.

"Give me a break, Conan!" Evan pleaded. "Why can't you leave me alone?"

Conan shrugged again. It was one of his favourite replies. His blue eyes twinkled merrily. "You're right, Evan," he said, his grin fading. "I shouldn't have tripped you."

"Yeah," Evan agreed, straightening his T-shirt.

"So you can pay me back," Conan offered.

"Huh?" Evan gaped at him.

Conan stuck out his massive chest. "Go ahead. Hit me in the stomach. I'll let you."

"Whoa. No way," Evan replied, trying to back away. He stumbled into a group of kids.

"Go ahead," Conan urged, following after him. "Hit me in the stomach. As hard as you can. It's only fair."

Evan studied his expression. "You really mean it?"

Conan nodded, tight-lipped. He stuck out his chest. "As hard as you can. Go ahead. I won't hit back. I promise."

Evan hesitated. Should he go ahead and do it?

I may never get a chance like this again, he thought.

14

A lot of kids were watching, Evan realized.

If I hit him really hard, if I hurt him, if I make him cry out—then maybe kids around here will have a little respect for me.

I'll be Evan the Giant Killer. The guy who pounded Conan the Barbarian.

He balled his hand into a tight fist and raised it.

"Is *that* your fist?" Conan cried, laughing.

Evan nodded.

"Oooh—this is going to hurt!" Conan cried sarcastically. He made his knees tremble.

Everyone laughed.

I may surprise him, Evan thought angrily.

"Go ahead. As hard as you can," Conan urged. He sucked in a deep breath and held it.

Evan pulled his arm back and swung his fist as hard as he could.

The fist made a solid *thud* as it hit Conan's stomach.

It felt like hitting a concrete wall.

Evan's hand throbbed with pain.

"Hey—!" a man's voice called angrily.

Startled, Evan spun around—to see Mr Murphy glaring at him.

"No fighting!" Mr Murphy yelled at Evan.

The teacher came bounding up to them and stepped between the two boys. Huffing for breath, he turned to Conan. "Why did Evan hit you?" he demanded.

Conan shrugged. His blue eyes went wide and innocent. "I don't know, Mr Murphy," he replied in a tiny, forlorn voice. "Evan just walked up and hit me as hard as he could."

Conan rubbed his stomach and uttered a short whimper. "Ow. He really hurt me."

Mr Murphy narrowed his beady black eyes at Evan. His chubby face turned bright red again. "Evan, I saw the whole thing. I really don't understand you," he said softly.

"But Mr Murphy—" Evan started.

The teacher raised a hand to silence him. "If you were angry about what happened in class," Mr Murphy said, "you shouldn't take it out on other kids."

Conan rubbed his stomach tenderly. "I hope Evan didn't *break* anything!" he murmured.

"Do you want to see the nurse?" Mr Murphy asked.

Conan shook his head. Evan could see he was

having trouble keeping a straight face. "I'll be okay," he said, and staggered away.

What a phony! Evan thought bitterly.

Did Conan know the whole time that Murphy was standing there? Probably.

"Go and take care of Cuddles," Mr Murphy told Evan, frowning. "And try to shape up, Evan. I'm going to be watching you."

Evan muttered a reply and trudged back into the classroom. Sunlight streamed in through the wall of windows. A strong breeze made the blind flap over the open window near the teacher's desk.

Feeling angry and upset, his stomach churning, Evan made his way through the empty room to the hamster cage. Cuddles wrinkled his nose in greeting. The hamster knew the routine by now.

Evan gazed into the metal cage at the brown-and-white creature. Why do people think hamsters are cute? he wondered.

Because they wrinkle their noses? Because they run around and around on wheels like total jerks? Because of their cute little buck teeth?

Cuddles stared up at him with his little black eyes.

He has Mr Murphy's eyes, Evan thought, chuckling to himself. Maybe that's why Murphy likes him so much.

"Okay, okay. So you're cute," Evan told the

17

hamster. "But I know your secret. You're just a big fat rat in disguise!"

Cuddles wrinkled his nose again in reply.

With a loud sigh, Evan went to work. Holding his breath because he hated the smell, he pulled out the bottom tray.

"You're a messy little guy," he told the hamster. "When are you going to learn to clean up your own room?"

Still holding his breath, he dumped out the old newspaper shavings and replaced them with fresh shavings from the box in the supply cupboard.

He returned the bottom tray to its place as Cuddles watched with great interest. Then he poured fresh water into the water bottle.

"How about some sunflower seeds?" Evan asked. He began to feel a little more cheerful, knowing his job was almost finished.

He removed the seed cup from the cage and made his way across the room to the supply closet to get fresh sunflower seeds.

"Okay, Cuddles," he called, "these look yummy!"

He started to carry the seeds back to the cage. Halfway across the room, Evan stopped and uttered a startled gasp.

The cage door hung wide open.

The hamster was gone.

A choking sound escaped Evan's lips as he stared at the empty cage.

His eyes darted frantically around the room. "Cuddles? Cuddles?" he called in a frightened voice.

Why am I yelling? he asked himself, spinning around in a total panic. The stupid hamster doesn't know its name!

He heard footsteps out in the hall.

Mr Murphy?

No, please—no! Evan pleaded silently.

Don't let it be Mr Murphy. Don't let him return until I have Cuddles safely back in his cage.

Cuddles was Mr Murphy's most precious possession. He had told this to the class time and again.

Evan knew that if anything happened to Cuddles, Mr Murphy would be on Evan's case for the rest of the year. No—for the rest of his *life*!

19

Evan froze in the centre of the room, listening hard.

The footsteps passed by the room.

Evan started breathing again.

"Cuddles? Where are you, Cuddles?" he called in a trembling voice. "I have some delicious sunflower seeds for you."

He spotted the furry, brown-and-white creature on the chalk tray under the front blackboard.

"There you are! I can see you!" Evan whispered, tiptoeing towards it.

Cuddles was busily chewing something. A small piece of white chalk.

Evan tiptoed closer. "I have seeds for you, Cuddles," he whispered. "Much tastier than chalk."

Cuddles held the stick of chalk in his front paws, turning it as he chewed.

Evan crept closer. Closer.

"Look. Seeds." He held the plastic seed cup out to the hamster.

Cuddles didn't look up.

Evan crept up closer. Closer.

Close enough to dive forward—

—and *miss*!

The hamster dropped the chalk and scampered down the chalk tray.

Evan made another frantic grab—and came up with nothing but air.

Letting out a frustrated groan, Evan saw the hamster dive to the floor and scamper behind Mr Murphy's desk. The hamster's feet skidded and slid on the linoleum floor, its toenails clicking loudly.

"You can't get away! You're too fat!" Evan cried. He dropped to his knees and peered under the desk.

He could see Cuddles staring back at him from the darkness. The animal was breathing rapidly, its sides swelling with each breath.

"Don't be scared," Evan whispered soothingly. "I'm going to put you back in your nice, safe cage."

He crawled quickly to the desk.

The hamster stared back at him, breathing hard. It didn't move—until Evan reached for it. Then Cuddles scampered away, his tiny paws sliding on the floor.

Evan jumped angrily to his feet. "Cuddles— what's your problem?" he demanded loudly. "This isn't a stupid game!"

It wasn't a game at all, Evan knew.

If he didn't get the hamster back in the cage, Mr Murphy would punish him for sure. Or suspend him from school. Or get his family kicked out of Atlanta!

Calm down, Evan urged himself. Don't panic.

He took a deep breath and held it.

21

Then he saw the hamster on the window ledge, just inside the open window.

Okay, Evan—go ahead and panic! he told himself.

This was definitely panic time.

He tried to call to the hamster. But his voice came out a choked whisper.

Swallowing hard, Evan edged slowly towards the window ledge.

"Come here, Cuddles," he whispered. "Please, Cuddles—come here."

Closer, closer.

Almost close enough to reach the hamster.

Almost close enough.

"Don't move, Cuddles. Don't move."

He reached out his hand slowly. Slowly.

Cuddles glanced back at him with his soft black eyes.

Then the hamster jumped out of the window.

Evan hung back for only a second.

Then he jumped out of the window after the hamster.

Luckily, the science classroom was on the ground floor. Evan landed face down in a low evergreen hedge. Struggling and squirming, it took him a while to climb to his feet.

He took several steps over the grass, then turned and stared back along the bottom of the long hedge. "Cuddles—are you under there?"

Evan squatted down to get a better view. The hedge stretched the entire length of the school building. Cuddles could hide under there for ever.

And if I don't find him, Evan told himself bitterly, I'd better hide under there for ever, too!

To the right, Evan could hear voices from the playground. Happy, shouting voices. Carefree voices.

Still squatting, he turned towards the happy

voices—and saw a fat brown ball wobbling over the grass towards the playground.

No. Not a ball. "Cuddles!"

That fat hamster isn't getting away this time! Evan decided, jumping up and starting to chase after the creature. I'll catch him if I have to *sit* on him!

A picture flashed into Evan's mind of Cuddles, flat as a pancake after Evan had sat upon him. A little, round, furry hamster rug.

Despite his panic, the thought of Cuddles as a rug brought a smile to Evan's perspiring face.

As he ran, he kept his eyes on Cuddles. The hamster was wobbling rapidly over the grass towards the playground.

"Oh, no!" Evan cried out in horror as Cuddles darted in front of two girls speeding across the grass on bikes.

Laughing together, they didn't even see the hamster.

Cuddles is about to be squashed! Evan thought, shrinking back. He shut his eyes and waited for the *squish*.

But the bikes rolled smoothly on. And when they had passed, Evan spotted Cuddles continuing his journey to the playground unharmed.

"Cuddles—come back here!" he shouted furiously.

The hamster appeared to speed up. He tumbled

on to the baseball diamond, all four paws scurrying over the dirt of the third-base line.

Several kids stopped their game to stare.

"Stop him! Grab the hamster!" Evan shouted desperately.

But the kids only laughed.

"Know how to catch him?" a joker named Robbie Greene called to Evan. "Make a sound like a sunflower seed!"

"That's an old joke!" a girl called to Robbie.

"Thanks for your help!" Evan shouted sarcastically. He ran over the pitching mound and had crossed second base when he realized he had lost sight of Cuddles.

He stopped and spun around, his heart thudding wildly in his chest. He searched the grass of the infield. "Where—where is he?" he stammered. "Can you see him?"

But the kids had returned to their softball game.

I can't lose him now! Evan told himself, choked with panic. I *can't*!

Sweat poured down Evan's forehead. He mopped it with one hand, brushing back his curly, red hair. His T-shirt clung wetly to his back. His mouth felt dry as cotton.

Jogging into the outfield, he searched the grass.

"Cuddles?"

No sign of him.

25

A round, brownish lump in the grass turned out to be someone's baseball glove.

"Cuddles?"

A kickball game was underway on the opposite diamond. Kids were shouting and cheering. Evan saw Bree Douglas, a girl from his class, slide hard into second base just before the ball.

"Has—has anyone seen Cuddles?" Evan gasped, trotting on to the diamond.

Kids turned to gawk at him.

"Out here?" Bree called, brushing off the knees of her jeans. "Evan, did you take the hamster out for a walk?"

Everyone laughed. Scornful laughter.

"He—he got away," Evan replied, panting.

"Is *this* what you're looking for?" a familiar voice called.

Evan turned to see Conan Barber, a pleased smile on his handsome face, his blue eyes gleaming.

Gripping it by its furry back, Conan held the hamster up in one hand. Cuddles's four legs scurried in mid-air.

"You—you caught him!" Evan cried gratefully. He let out a long sigh of relief. "He jumped out of the window."

Evan reached out both hands for the hamster, but Conan jerked Cuddles out of his reach. "Prove it's yours," Conan said, grinning.

"Huh?"

"Can you identify it?" Conan demanded, his eyes burning into Evan's, challenging Evan. "Prove this hamster is yours."

Evan swallowed hard and glanced around.

Kids from the kickball game were huddling near. They were all grinning, delighted with Conan's nasty joke.

Evan sighed wearily and reached again for the hamster.

But Conan was at least a foot taller than Evan. He lifted the hamster high above Evan's head, out of Evan's reach.

"Prove it's yours," he repeated, flashing the others a grin.

"Give me a break, Conan," Evan pleaded. "I've been chasing this stupid hamster for hours. I just want to get him back in his cage before Mr Murphy—"

"Do you have a licence for him?" Conan demanded, still holding the squirming hamster above Evan's head. "Show me the licence."

Evan jumped and stretched both hands up, trying to grab Cuddles away.

But Conan was too fast for him. He dodged away. Evan grabbed air.

Some kids laughed.

"Give him the hamster, Conan," Bree called. She hadn't moved from second base.

Conan's cold blue eyes sparkled excitedly. "I'll

tell you how you can get the hamster back," he told Evan.

"Huh?" Evan glared at him. He was getting really tired of Conan's game.

"Here's how to get old Cuddles back," Conan continued, holding the hamster tightly against his chest in one hand and petting its back with the other. "Sing a song for it."

"Hey—no way!" Evan snapped. "Give it to me, Conan!"

Evan could feel his face growing even hotter. His knees started to tremble. He hoped no one could see it.

"Sing 'Row, Row, Row Your Boat' and I'll give you Cuddles. Promise," Conan said, smirking.

Some kids laughed. They moved closer, eager to see what Evan would do.

Evan shook his head. "No way."

"Come on," Conan urged softly, stroking the hamster's brown fur. "'Row, Row, Row Your Boat'. Just a few choruses. You know how it goes, don't you?"

More cruel laughter from the others.

Conan's grin grew wider. "Come on, Evan. You like to sing, don't you?"

"No, I *hate* singing," Evan muttered, his eyes on Cuddles.

"Hey, don't be modest," Conan insisted. "I'll bet you're a great singer. Are you a soprano or an alto?"

Loud laughter.

Evan's hands tightened into hard fists at his sides. He wanted to punch Conan, and punch him and punch him. He wanted to wipe the grin off Conan's handsome face with his fists.

But he remembered what it had felt like to punch Conan. It had felt like hitting the side of a truck.

He took a deep breath. "If I sing the stupid song, will you really give me back the hamster?"

Conan didn't reply.

Evan suddenly realized that Conan wasn't looking at him any more. No one was. They had all raised their eyes over Evan's shoulder.

Confused, Evan spun around—to face Mr Murphy.

"What is going on here?" the teacher demanded, his tiny black eyes moving from Evan to Conan, then back to Evan.

Before Evan could reply, Conan held up the hamster. "Here's Cuddles, Mr Murphy," Conan said. "Evan let him get away. But I rescued Cuddles just as he was going to get run over."

Mr Murphy let out a horrified gasp. "Run over?" he cried. "Cuddles? Run over?"

The teacher reached out his chubby pink hands and took the hamster from Conan. He held the hamster against his bulging shirt and petted it, making soothing sounds to it.

"Thank you, Conan," Mr Murphy said after calming Cuddles. He glared at Evan. "I'm very disappointed in you, Evan."

Evan started to defend himself. But Mr Murphy raised a hand to silence him. "We'll talk about it tomorrow. Right now I must get poor Cuddles back into his cage."

Evan slumped to the ground. He watched Mr Murphy carry the hamster back to the school building. Mr Murphy waddles just like the hamster, Evan realized.

Normally, that thought would have cheered him up.

But Evan was far too unhappy to be cheered up by anything.

Conan had embarrassed him in front of all the others. And the big, grinning hulk had managed to get Evan in trouble with Mr Murphy *twice* in one afternoon!

The kickball game had started up again. Evan climbed slowly to his feet and began trudging to the school building to get his backpack.

He couldn't decide who he hated more—Cuddles or Conan.

He had a sudden picture of Cuddles stuffed inside a muffin tin, being baked in an oven.

Even that lovely thought didn't cheer Evan up.

He pulled his backpack out of the locker and slung it over his shoulder. Then he slammed the locker shut, the sound clanging down the empty corridor.

He pushed open the front door and headed for home, walking slowly, lost in his unhappy thoughts.

What a horrible day, he told himself. At least nothing *worse* could happen to me today.

He had just crossed the street and was making his way on the pavement in front of a tall hedge—when someone leaped out at him, grabbed his shoulders hard from behind, and pulled him roughly to the ground.

Evan let out a frightened cry and gazed into his attacker's face. "*You!*" he cried.

"Here's a little advice, Evan," Andy said, grinning down at him. "Don't go for the wrestling team."

"Andy!" Evan cried, staring up at her in surprise. "What are *you* doing here?"

She reached out both hands and helped tug him to his feet. Then she tossed back her short, brown hair with a flick of her head. Her brown eyes flashed excitedly.

"Didn't you read any of my letters?" she demanded.

Evan had met Andy that summer, when he'd stayed with his great-aunt for a few weeks. He and Andy had become good friends.

She was with him when he bought the container of Monster Blood. She shared the whole frightening Monster Blood adventure with him.

Evan liked Andy because she was funny, and fearless, and kind of crazy. He could never predict what she would do next!

She didn't even dress like other girls Evan knew. Andy loved bright colours. Right now she was wearing a sleeveless magenta T-shirt over bright yellow shorts, which matched her yellow trainers.

"I *told* you in my last letter that my parents were sent overseas for a year," Andy said, giving Evan a playful shove. "I *told* you they were sending me to Atlanta to live with my aunt and uncle. I *told* you I'd be living just three streets away from you!"

"I know. I know," Evan replied, rolling his eyes. "I just didn't expect to see you jump out of the hedge at me."

"Why not?" Andy demanded, her dark eyes exploring his.

Evan didn't know how to answer that question.

"Glad to see me?" Andy asked.

"No," he joked.

She pulled up a thick blade of grass and stuck it in the corner of her mouth. They began walking toward Evan's house.

"I'm starting at your school on Monday," she told him, chewing on the blade of grass.

"Thrills and chills," he replied, snickering.

She shoved him off the pavement. "I thought people were supposed to be polite in the South."

"I'm new here," Evan replied.

"How's Trigger?" she asked, kicking a pebble across the pavement.

"Good," Evan told her.

"Like to talk a lot?" she asked sarcastically.

"I'm in a bad mood," he confessed. "It hasn't been the greatest day."

"It *couldn't* be as bad as the day the Monster Blood went berserk!" Andy exclaimed.

Evan groaned. "Don't mention Monster Blood to me. Please!"

She studied him. Her expression turned serious. "What's wrong, Evan? You look really upset," she said. "Don't you like it here?"

He shook his head. "Not much."

As they walked, he told her about all the trouble he was having in his new school. He told her about Mr Murphy and Cuddles, and how the teacher was always on his case.

And he told her about Conan the Barbarian, and how Conan was always picking on him, always getting him into trouble, always playing tricks on him and making him look bad.

"And no one will believe me about the Monster Blood," Evan added.

They were standing at the bottom of his drive. They glanced up at Evan's new house, a two-storey red brick house with a sloping red tile roof. The late afternoon sun dipped behind a large puff of cloud, and a broad shadow rolled across the lawn.

Andy's mouth dropped open. The blade of grass fell out. "You *told* people about the Monster Blood?" she asked in surprise.

Evan nodded. "Yeah, why not? It's a cool story, isn't it?"

"And you expected people to *believe* you?" Andy cried, slapping her forehead. "Didn't they just think you were *weird*?"

"Yeah," Evan replied bitterly. "They all think I'm weird."

Andy laughed. "Well, you *are* weird!"

"Thanks a bunch, Annnndrea!" Evan muttered. He knew she hated to be called by her real name.

"Don't call me Andrea," she replied sharply. She raised a fist. "I'll pound you."

"Annnnnndrea," he repeated. He ducked away as she swung her fist. "You punch like a girl!" he exclaimed.

"You'll *bleed* like a boy!" she threatened, laughing.

He stopped. He suddenly had an idea. "Hey— you can tell everyone I'm not weird!"

"Huh? Why would I do that?" Andy demanded.

"No. Really," Evan said excitedly. "You can tell everyone at school that the Monster Blood was real. That you were there. That you saw it."

Andy's expression suddenly changed. Her dark eyes lit up, and a sly grin crossed her face. "I can do better than that," she said mysteriously.

Evan grabbed her shoulder. "Huh? What do you mean? What do you mean you can do better?"

"You'll see," she replied, teasing him. "I brought something with me."

"What? What is it? What do you mean?" Evan demanded.

"Meet me tomorrow after school," she told him. "At that little park over there."

She pointed to the next street. A narrow park, only a hundred metres long, ran along the bank of a shallow stream.

"But what *is* it?" Evan cried.

She laughed. "I *love* torturing you!" she declared. "But it's a little too easy."

Then she turned and headed down the street, running at full speed.

"Andy—wait!" Evan called. "What have you got? What did you bring?"

She didn't even turn round.

Evan dreamed about Monster Blood that night.

He dreamed about it nearly every night.

Tonight he dreamed that his dad had eaten a glob of it. Now Mr Ross wanted to go to his office, but he had grown too big to fit through the door.

"You're in trouble now, Evan!" Mr Ross bellowed, making the whole house shake. "Big trouble!"

Big trouble.

The words stuck in Evan's mind as he sat up in bed and tried to shake away the dream.

The curtains flapped silently in front of his open bedroom window. Pale yellow stars dotted the charcoal sky. Staring hard, Evan could see the Great Bear. Or was it the Little Bear? He never could remember.

Shutting his eyes and settling back on the pillow, Evan thought about Andy. He was glad she had come to stay in Atlanta for a while. She could be a real pain. But she was also a lot of fun.

What did she want to show him in the park after school?

Probably nothing, Evan decided. It was probably just a silly joke. Andy loved silly jokes.

How can I get her to tell the kids at school about Monster Blood? he wondered. How can I get Andy to tell everyone that I didn't make it up, that it's true?

He was still thinking about this problem as he fell back into a restless sleep.

The next day at school wasn't much better than the last.

Somehow, during free reading period, Conan had crept under the table and tied Evan's laces together. When Evan got up to go to the water fountain, he fell flat on his face. He scraped a knee, but no one cared. The kids laughed for hours.

"Evan's mummy tied his shoes funny this morning!" Conan told everyone. And they laughed even harder.

In science class, Mr Murphy called Evan over to the hamster cage. "Look at poor Cuddles," the teacher said, shaking his round head solemnly.

Evan peered down into the metal cage. Cuddles was curled up in a corner under a pile of shavings. The hamster was trembling and breathing in short gasps.

"Poor Cuddles has been like that ever since

yesterday," Mr Murphy told Evan with an accusing frown. "Cuddles is sick because of your carelessness."

"I—I'm sorry," Evan stammered. He stared hard at the quivering hamster. You're faking—aren't you, Cuddles? Evan thought. You're faking just to get me in trouble!

The hamster twitched and stared up at him with mournful, black eyes.

When Evan sat back down in his seat, he felt cold water seep through the back of his jeans. With a startled cry, he jumped right back up. Someone—probably Conan—had poured a cup of water on his chair.

That had the class laughing for at least ten minutes. They stopped only when Mr Murphy threatened to keep everyone after school.

"Sit down, Evan," the teacher ordered.

"But, Mr Murphy—" Evan started.

"Sit down—now!" Mr Murphy insisted.

Evan dropped back down into the wet chair. What choice did he have?

Andy was waiting for Evan by the trickling brown stream that rolled through the tiny park. The old sassafras trees bent and whispered in a hot breeze. A tall Georgia pine leaned over the water as if trying to reach across the stream.

Andy was wearing a bright blue T-shirt over lime-green cycling shorts. She had been staring at her reflection in the muddy water. She spun around smiling as Evan called to her.

"Hey, how's it going?" he called. He stepped up beside her and dropped his backpack to the ground.

"How was school?" Andy asked.

"Same as always," Evan replied, sighing. Then, his expression brightened. "What did you bring?" he asked eagerly.

"You'll see." She clamped a hand over his eyes. "Shut your eyes, Evan. And don't open them until I say."

He obediently shut his eyes. But when she pulled her hand away, he opened them a tiny crack, just enough to see. He watched her go behind the pine tree and pick up a small brown paper bag.

She carried the bag over to him. "You're peeking—aren't you!" she accused him.

"Maybe," he confessed, grinning.

She punched him playfully in the stomach. He cried out and his eyes shot open. "What's in the bag?"

Grinning, Andy handed the bag to him.

He pulled it open, peered inside—and his mouth dropped open in shock.

The familiar blue can, about the size of a can of soup.

"Andy—you—you—" Evan stammered, still staring wide-eyed into the bag.

He reached in and pulled out the plastic can.

He read the faded label: MONSTER BLOOD.

Then he read the words in tiny type below it: SURPRISING MIRACLE SUBSTANCE.

"I saved it," Andy said, beaming proudly.

Evan couldn't get over his shock. "You brought Monster Blood! I don't believe it! You brought Monster Blood!"

"No." She shook her head. "It's empty, Evan. The can is empty."

His face fell. He sighed in total disappointment.

"But you can show the can to everyone," Andy insisted. "That will prove you didn't make it up. It will prove that Monster Blood really exists."

Evan sighed again. "What good is an empty can?" he groaned.

He pulled off the top, peered inside—and screamed.

With a trembling hand, Evan tilted the can so that Andy could see inside.

"Oh, no!" she shrieked, pulling her hands to her cheeks.

The can was half full.

Inside, a green glob of gooey Monster Blood shimmered in the sunlight like lime jelly.

"But it was *empty*!" Andy protested, staring into the can. "I *know* it was!"

Evan shook the can. The green glob inside quivered.

"There must have been a tiny speck in there," Evan guessed. "Down at the bottom of the can. And now it's growing and growing again."

"Great!" Andy declared. She slapped him on the back so hard, he nearly dropped the blue can.

"Great? What's so great?" he demanded shakily.

"Now you can show this to the kids at your

school," she replied. "Now they'll *have* to believe you."

"I suppose," Evan replied in a low voice.

"Oh! I have a better idea!" she exclaimed, her dark eyes lighting up mischievously.

"Uh-oh," Evan moaned.

"Slip a little glob of it in that guy Conan's lunch tomorrow. When he starts to grow as big as a hippo, everyone will see that Monster Blood is real."

"No way!" Evan cried. He cupped the blue can in both hands, as if protecting it from Andy. "Conan is already big enough!" he told her, taking a step back. "I don't want him to grow another inch. Do you know what he could *do* to me if he became a giant?"

Andy laughed and shrugged. "It was just an idea."

"A *bad* idea," Evan said sharply. "A really bad idea."

"You're no fun," she teased. She leaped forward and tried to wrestle the can from his hands.

He spun around, turning his back to her, and hunched over, protecting the can.

"Give it to me!" she cried, laughing. She started tickling his sides. "Give it! Give it!"

"No!" he protested, breaking free. He ran to the safety of a tall evergreen shrub.

"It's mine!" Andy declared, coming after him,

hands at her waist. "If you're not going to use it, hand it back."

Evan stood his ground. His expression turned serious. "Andy, don't you remember?" he demanded shrilly. "Don't you remember how scary this stuff was? Don't you remember how dangerous it was? All the trouble it caused?"

"So?" she replied, her eyes on the blue can.

"We have to get rid of it," Evan told her firmly. "We can't let it out of the can. It will grow and grow and never stop."

"But I thought you wanted to show it to the kids to prove that it's real."

"No," Evan interrupted. "I changed my mind. This stuff is too dangerous. We *have* to get rid of it." He locked his eyes on hers, his features tight with fear. "Andy, I've had nightmares every night because of this stuff. I don't want any *new* nightmares."

"Okay, okay," she muttered. She kicked at an upraised tree root. Then she handed him the brown paper bag.

Evan clicked the top back on the can of Monster Blood. Then he shoved the can into the bag. "Now how do we get rid of it?" he wondered out loud.

"I know. Dump it in the stream," Andy suggested.

Evan shook his head. "No good. What if it gets out and pollutes the stream?"

"This stream is *already* polluted!" Andy exclaimed. "It's just a big mud puddle!"

"It isn't deep enough," Evan insisted. "Someone will find the can and pull it out. We can't take a chance."

"Then how do we get rid of it?" Andy asked, twisting her face in concentration. "Hmmmm. We could eat it ourselves. *That* would get rid of it!"

"Very funny," Evan muttered, rolling his eyes.

"Just trying to be helpful," Andy said.

"You're about as helpful as toothache!" Evan shot back.

"Ha-ha. Remind me to laugh at that sometime," she replied, sticking her tongue out at him.

"How can we get rid of it?" Evan repeated, gripping the bag in both hands. "How?"

"I know!" a boy's voice called, startling them both.

Conan Barber stepped out from behind a tall shrub.

"You can give it to me!" he declared. He reached out a big, powerful-looking hand to grab the bag.

Evan swung the paper bag behind his back.

Conan lumbered towards them over the tall grass. His eyes were narrowed menacingly at Evan.

How long has he been hiding there? Evan wondered. Did he hear us talk about the Monster Blood? Is that why he wants the bag?

"Hi, I'm Andy," Andy chirped brightly. She stepped in between the two boys and flashed Conan a smile.

"Andy is a boy's name," Conan said, making a disgusted face. He turned his hard stare on her, challenging her.

"And what kind of a name is Conan?" Andy shot back, returning his stare.

"You *know* me?" Conan asked, sounding surprised.

"You're famous," Andy replied dryly.

Conan suddenly remembered Evan. He stuck out his big paw. "I'll take the bag now."

"Why should I give it to you?" Evan demanded, trying to keep his voice calm and steady.

"Because it's mine," Conan lied. "I dropped it here."

"You dropped an empty bag here?" Evan asked.

Conan swatted a fly from his blond hair. "It isn't empty. I saw you put something in it. Hand it over. Now."

"Well . . . okay." Evan handed him the paper bag. Conan eagerly reached inside.

His hand came out empty.

He peered inside the bag. Empty.

He stared hard at Andy, then at Evan.

"I *told* you it was empty," Evan said.

"Suppose I made a mistake," Conan muttered. "Hey, no hard feelings. Shake." Conan reached out his big right hand to Evan.

Evan reluctantly stuck out his hand.

Conan slid his hand over Evan's and began to tighten his grip. Harder. Harder.

Evan's fingers cracked so loudly, they sounded like a tree falling!

Conan squeezed Evan's hand harder and harder until Evan screamed in pain. When Conan finally let go, the hand looked like a slab of raw hamburger.

"Nice handshake you got there!" Conan exclaimed, grinning.

47

He snapped his finger against Andy's nose, then headed off quickly towards the street, taking long strides, laughing to himself.

"Great guy," Andy muttered, rubbing her nose.

Evan blew on his hand, as if trying to put out a fire. "Maybe I can learn to be left-handed," he murmured.

"Hey—where's the Monster Blood?" Andy demanded.

"I—I dropped it," Evan replied, still examining his hand.

"Huh?" She kicked away a clump of weeds and stepped over to him.

"I thought I could shove the can into my back jeans pocket while Conan was talking to you," Evan explained. "But it slipped out of my hand. I dropped it."

He turned, bent over, and picked it up from the tall grass. "Good thing it didn't roll or anything. Conan would have seen it."

"He wouldn't know what to do with it if he had it," Andy said.

"What are *we* going to do with it?" Evan demanded. "It's already caused us trouble. We've got to hide it, or throw it away, or—or—"

He pulled open the lid. "Oh, wow! Look!" He held the can up to Andy's face. The green goo had grown nearly to the top of the can. "It's starting to grow a lot faster. I expect because we exposed it to the air."

Evan slammed the lid on tight.

"Let's bury it," Andy suggested. "Here. Right under this tree. We'll dig a deep hole and bury it."

Evan liked the idea. It was simple and quick.

They squatted down and began digging with their hands. The dirt beneath the tree was soft. The hole grew deep before they had worked up a sweat.

Evan dropped the blue can of Monster Blood into the hole. Then they quickly covered it with dirt, smoothing it out until it was impossible to tell a hole had been dug.

"This was a good plan," Andy said, climbing to her feet, playfully wiping the dirt off her hands on the back of Evan's T-shirt. "If we need it, we'll know where it is."

Evan's red hair was matted to his forehead with sweat. He had a wide smear of dirt across his freckled forehead. "Huh? Why would we need it?" he demanded.

Andy shrugged. "You never know."

"We won't need it," Evan told her firmly. "We won't."

He was very, very wrong.

"Hey, Dad, what's up?" Evan stepped into the garage.

Mr Ross stopped hammering and turned round. He smiled at Evan. "Want to see my newest work?"

"Yeah. Sure," Evan replied. Every weekend, his father spent hour after hour in his garage workshop, banging away on large sheets of metal, making what he called his "works".

He chiselled and hammered and sawed, and put a lot of effort into his sculptures. But to Evan, they all looked like banged-up sheets of metal when they were finished.

Mr Ross took a few steps back to admire his current project. He lowered his heavy mallet in one hand and pointed with the chisel he held in his other hand. "I used brass for this one," he told Evan. "I call it 'Autumn Leaf'."

Evan studied it thoughtfully. "It looks like a leaf," he lied. It looks like Dad ruined a perfectly good piece of brass, he thought, trying to keep a straight face.

"It's not supposed to look like a leaf," Mr Ross corrected Evan. "It's supposed to look like my *impression* of a leaf."

"Oh." Evan scratched his curly, red hair as he studied it some more. "Neat, Dad," he said. "I see what you mean."

Then something else caught his eye. "Hey— what's this?"

Evan carefully stepped over several jagged, bent shards of metal. He made his way to another metal sculpture and ran his hand over the smooth, shiny surface. It was an enormous aluminium cylinder that rested above a flat wooden base.

"Go ahead. Spin it," Mr Ross instructed, smiling proudly.

Evan pushed the cylinder with both hands. It spun slowly over the wooden base.

"I call it 'The Wheel'," his father told him.

Evan laughed. "That's cool, Dad. You invented the wheel!"

"Don't laugh!" Mr Ross replied, grinning. "That sculpture was accepted at the annual arts competition at your school. I have to take it to the auditorium later this week."

Evan gave "The Wheel" another spin. "I'll bet no one else made a wheel that really spins," he told his father. "You can't lose with this, Dad," he teased.

"Sarcasm is the lowest form of humour," Mr Ross muttered with a frown.

Evan said goodbye and made his way out of the garage, stepping carefully over the jagged pieces of brass and tin. As he headed to the house, he could hear the *clang clang clang* as his dad hammered away on his impression of a leaf.

In the halls after school on Monday, Evan hurried around a corner and bumped right into Andy. "I can't talk now," he told her breathlessly. "I'm late for basketball tryouts."

He glanced down the long hall. It was nearly empty. The gym door opened, and he could hear the *thump* of basketballs against the floor.

"How come you're late?" Andy demanded, blocking his path.

"Murphy kept me after class," Evan told her with a groan. "He put me on permanent hamster duty. I have to take care of Cuddles every afternoon for the rest of my life."

"Bad news," Andy murmured.

"No. That's the *good* news," Evan replied bitterly.

"What's the *bad* news?"

"The bad news is that Mr Murphy is also the basketball coach!"

"Well, good luck," she said. "Hope you make the team."

Evan ran past her, his heart pounding.

Mr Murphy is such a rat, he thought unhappily. He'll probably keep me off the team because I'm late to practice—even though it's *his* fault I'm late!

Evan took a deep breath. No. Stop thinking like that, he scolded himself.

Think positive. I've got to think positive.

Sure, I'm not as tall as the other guys. Maybe I'm not as big or as strong. But I'm a good basketball player. And I can make this team.

I can make this team. I know I can!

Having finished his pep talk to himself, Evan pulled open the double gym doors and stepped into the huge, brightly lit gym.

"Think fast!" a voice called.

Evan felt his face explode with pain.

Then everything went black.

When Evan opened his eyes, he found himself
staring up at about twenty guys and Mr
Murphy.

He was stretched out flat on his back on the
gym floor. His face still hurt. A lot.

He reached a hand up and touched his nose. To
his dismay, it felt like a wilted leaf of lettuce.

"You okay, Evan?" Mr Murphy asked quietly.
As the teacher leaned over Evan, the whistle
that was on a string around his neck bumped
against Evan's chest.

"Did my face explode?" Evan asked weakly.

Some of the guys snickered. Mr Murphy
glowered at them angrily. Then he turned back
to Evan. "Conan hit you in the face with the
basketball," he reported.

"He's got bad reflexes, Coach," Evan heard
Conan say from somewhere above him. "He
should've caught the ball. I really thought he'd
catch it. But he's got bad reflexes."

"I saw the whole thing," Conan's friend, a huge hulk of a kid named Biggie Malick, chimed in. "It wasn't Conan's fault. Evan should've caught the ball. It was a perfect pass."

Perfect, Evan thought with a sigh. He touched his nose again. This time, it felt like a lump of mashed potatoes. At least it isn't broken, he thought glumly.

Evan's basketball tryout went downhill from there.

Mr Murphy helped him to his feet. "Are you sure you want to try out?" he asked.

Thanks for the support, Evan thought bitterly.

"I think I can make the team," he said.

But Conan, Biggie, and the other guys had other ideas.

During the ball-handling tryout, Evan confidently began dribbling across the floor. Halfway to the basket, Biggie bumped him hard—and Conan stole the ball away.

They blocked Evan's shots. They stole his passes.

They bumped him every time he moved, sending him sprawling to the hardwood floor again and again.

A fast pass from Conan caught Evan in the mouth.

"Oops! Sorry!" Conan yelled.

Biggie laughed like a hyena.

"Defence! I want to see defence!" Mr Murphy shouted from the sidelines.

Evan lowered himself into a defensive stance. As Conan dribbled the ball towards him, Evan prepared to defend the basket.

Conan drove closer. Closer.

Evan raised both hands to block Conan's shot.

But to Evan's surprise, Conan let the ball bounce away. In one swift motion, he grabbed Evan by the waist, leaped high in the air, and stuffed Evan into the basket.

"Three points!" Conan shouted in triumph.

Biggie and the other guys rushed to congratulate Conan, laughing and cheering.

Mr Murphy had to get a stepladder to help Evan down.

His hand on Evan's shoulder, the teacher led him to the side. "You're just not tall enough, Evan," he said, rubbing his pink chins. "Don't take it personally. Maybe you'll grow. But for now, you're just not tall enough."

Evan didn't say a word. He lowered his head and sadly slumped out of the gym.

Conan came running up to him at the door. "Hey, Evan, no hard feelings," he said. He stuck out his big, sweaty hand. "Shake."

Evan held up his hand to show Andy.

"It looks like a wilted petunia," she said.

"I can't believe I fell for Conan's stupid

handshake trick twice!" Evan wailed.

It was the next afternoon. Evan and Andy had walked from school to the small park near their houses. Evan had complained about Mr Murphy and Conan and the other basketball players the whole way.

The late afternoon sun beamed down on them as they walked. Andy stopped to watch two monarch butterflies, their black-and-gold wings fluttering majestically as they hovered over a patch of blue and yellow wildflowers along the creekbed.

Even the trickling brown stream looked pretty on this bright day. Tiny white gnats sparkled like diamonds in the sunlight over the shimmering water.

Evan kicked at a fallen tree branch. Everything looked dark to him today.

Dark and ugly.

"It just wasn't fair," he grumbled, kicking the branch again. "It wasn't a fair tryout. Mr Murphy should have given me a better chance."

Andy tsk-tsked, her eyes on the sparkling creek.

"Someone should teach Mr Murphy a lesson," Evan said. "I wish I could think of some way of paying him back. I really do."

Andy turned to him. A devilish grin crossed her face. "I have a plan," she said softly. "A really good plan."

"What is it?" Evan demanded.

"What's your idea?" Evan demanded again.

Andy grinned at him. She was wearing a long, lime-green T-shirt over a Day-Glo orange T-shirt, pulled down over baggy blue shorts. The sunlight made all the colours so bright, Evan felt like shielding his eyes.

"You might not like it," Andy said coyly.

"Try me," Evan replied. "Come on. Don't keep me in suspense."

"Well . . ." Her eyes wandered over to the tree where they had buried the Monster Blood. "It has to do with the Monster Blood," she said reluctantly.

He swallowed hard. "That's okay. Go on."

"Well, it's a pretty simple plan. First, we dig up the Monster Blood," Andy said, watching his reaction.

"Yeah?"

"Then we take some to school," she continued.

"Yeah?"

58

"Then we feed it to Cuddles."

Evan's mouth dropped open.

"Just a little bit!" Andy quickly explained. "We feed Cuddles a tiny glob of it. Just enough to make him the size of a dog."

Evan laughed. It was a terrible idea, a truly evil idea—but he loved it!

He slapped Andy on the back. "You're bad, Andy!" he cried. "You're really bad!"

Andy grinned proudly. "I know."

Evan laughed again. "Could you see the look on Murphy's face when he comes in and sees his precious little hamster has grown as big as a cocker spaniel? What a riot!"

"So you'll do it?" Andy asked.

Evan's smile faded. "I think so," he replied thoughtfully. "If you promise we'll only use a tiny bit. And we'll bury the rest right away."

"Promise," Andy said. "Just enough to play our little joke on Mr Murphy. Then we'll never see the stuff again."

"Okay," Evan agreed.

They shook hands solemnly.

Then they hurried to the tree. Evan searched the entire park, squinting against the bright sunlight. He wanted to make sure no one was spying on them this time.

When he was sure the park was empty, he and Andy dropped to their knees under the tree and began scooping the dirt off the hole with their hands.

They had dug nearly two feet down when they realized the hole was empty.

"The Monster Blood!" Evan cried. "It—it's gone!"

"We must be digging under the wrong tree," Evan said, sweat pouring down his freckled forehead.

Andy pushed a wet strand of brown hair off her face with a dirt-covered finger. "No way." She shook her head. "This is the right tree. And the right hole."

"Then where is the Monster Blood?" Evan demanded shrilly.

They both came up with the answer to his question at the same time: "Conan!"

"He must have watched us bury it," Evan said, his eyes darting around the park as if he expected to see Conan jump out from behind a bush. "I *thought* he hurried away awfully fast that afternoon. He *knew* the paper bag wasn't empty."

Andy agreed. "He hid and watched us bury it. Then he waited till we were gone, and dug it up."

They both stared into the empty hole in horrified silence.

Andy broke the silence. "What is Conan going to do with it?" she asked, her voice just above a whisper.

"Probably eat it so he can grow bigger and pound me harder," Evan replied bitterly.

"But he doesn't know what Monster Blood does," Andy said. "He doesn't know how dangerous it is."

"Of course he does. I told him all about it," Evan replied. He slammed his hand against the tree trunk. "We have to get it back!"

Before science class the next afternoon, Evan found Conan in the hall. He and Biggie were standing next to Evan's locker. They were laughing loudly about something, slapping each other high-fives.

Conan wore a tight blue muscle shirt and baggy faded denim jeans with enormous holes at the knees. Biggie had wavy brown hair down to his shoulders. He wore a sleeveless white T-shirt and tight-fitting black denims.

They look like a couple of wrestlers! Evan thought as he stepped between them.

"Hey, look—it's Air Evan!" Conan joked. "King of basketball!"

He and Biggie guffawed loudly. Conan gave

Evan a slap on the back that sent him sprawling into Biggie.

"Uh...Conan? Did you find something in the park?" Evan asked, struggling to regain his balance.

Conan narrowed his eyes at Evan and didn't reply.

"Did you find something that belongs to Andy and me?" Evan repeated.

"You mean like your *brains*?" Conan exclaimed. He and his wrestling partner roared with laughter over that gem.

"Why don't we dribble him to class?" Biggie asked Conan. "Coach Murphy would like to see us get in some extra practice."

Conan laughed gleefully at that idea.

"Ha-ha. Very funny," Evan said sarcastically. "Look, Conan—that stuff you took. It's really dangerous. You have to give it back."

Conan opened his eyes in wide-eyed innocence. "I really don't know what you're talking about, Evan. Did you lose something?"

"You *know* I lost something," Evan replied sharply. "And I want it back."

Conan flashed a sly grin at Biggie. Then he turned back to Evan, his expression hardening. "I don't know what you mean, Evan," he said. "Really. I don't know what you and that girl lost. But tell you what. I'm a nice guy. I'll help you look for it."

He grabbed Evan around the waist with both hands. Biggie pulled Evan's locker door open.

"I'll help you look for it in your locker," Conan said.

He shoved Evan inside the locker and slammed the door shut.

Evan started pounding on the metal door, shouting for help.

But the bell had rung. Evan knew the corridor was empty. There was no one to hear his cries.

He decided to try fiddling with the latch. But it was too dark to see anything. And he was so jammed in, he couldn't raise his arms.

Finally, two girls happened to walk by, and they pulled open the locker door.

Evan came bursting out, red-faced, gasping for air.

The girls' laughter followed him all the way to Mr Murphy's class. "You're late," the teacher said sternly, glancing up at the wall clock as Evan staggered in.

Evan tried to explain why. But all that escaped his lips was a whistling breeze.

"I'm really tired of you disrupting my class, Evan," Mr Murphy said, rubbing his nearly bald head. "I'm afraid I'll be seeing you after school again. You can give Cuddles's cage a double cleaning. And while you're at it, you can scrub the blackboard and clean out all the test tubes, too."

"It's so dark," Evan whispered.

"It usually gets dark at night," Andy replied, rolling her eyes.

"The streetlight is out," Evan said, pointing. "And there's no moon tonight. That's why it's so dark."

"Hide!" Andy whispered.

They ducked behind the hedge as a car rolled slowly past. Evan shut his eyes as the white headlights moved over him. When the car turned the corner, they climbed to their feet.

It was a little after eight o'clock. They were standing in the street in front of Conan's house. Leaning against the low hedge, they stared across the sloping front lawn into the large window in the front of the house.

The lamp in the living room was lit, casting a dim rectangle of orange light that spilled into the front garden. The old trees at the sides of the small brick house whispered in a hot breeze.

"Are we really doing this?" Evan asked, huddling close to Andy. "Are we really going to break into Conan's house?"

"We're not going to *break* in," Andy whispered. "We're going to *sneak* in."

"But what if the Monster Blood isn't there?"

Evan asked, hoping she couldn't see his knees trembling.

"We *have* to look, don't we?" Andy shot back. She turned to study his face. He saw that she was frightened, too. "The Monster Blood will be there," she told him. "It's *got* to be."

Bending low, she started to creep across the dark garden to the house.

Evan hung back. "You checked it out?" he called to her. "Everyone is really gone?"

"His parents left right after dinner," Andy told him. "Then I saw Conan go out about ten minutes ago."

"Where?" Evan demanded.

"How should I know?" she asked sharply, putting her hands on her waist. "He left. The house is empty." She came back and tugged Evan's arm. "Come on. Let's sneak into Conan's room, get the Monster Blood, and get out of here!"

"I can't believe we're doing this," Evan said, sighing. "We—we could be arrested!"

"It was *your* idea!" Andy reminded him.

"Oh. Yeah. Right." He took a deep breath and held it, hoping it would help calm him down. "If we don't find it right away, we get out of there—right?"

"Right," Andy agreed. "Now come on." She gave him a little shove toward the house.

They took a few steps over the dew-wet grass.

They both stopped when they heard the low barking.

Andy grabbed Evan's arm.

The barking grew louder. They could hear the dog's heavy paws pounding the ground, approaching fast.

Two angry eyes. A loud warning bark. Another.

The dog attacked at full speed.

"Run!" Evan cried. "Conan has a guard dog!"

"Too late to run!" Andy shrieked.

The dog barked again.

Evan cried out and threw up his hands as the dog leaped for his throat.

The dog wasn't as big as Evan had thought—but it was strong.

It licked his face, pressing its wet snout into his cheek.

It licked his chin. And then his lips.

"Yuck!" Evan cried, laughing. "Trigger—how did you get here?"

Evan pulled the cocker spaniel off him and lowered it to the ground. Its stubby tail wagging furiously, Trigger started jumping on Andy.

"Your stupid dog scared me to death," she moaned.

"Me, too," Evan admitted. "I didn't hear him following us, did you?"

Andy squatted down and gave Trigger a few quick pats. Then she glanced down the street.

"Let's get inside," she said. "Conan or his parents could be back any minute."

Trigger pranced along as they made their way over the grass to the front door. The house loomed much bigger and darker as they crept up the steps.

"Down, Trigger. Stay down," Evan whispered. "You can't come in with us."

Andy tried the front door. "Locked."

Evan groaned. "Now what?"

"We try the back door, of course," Andy replied. She had already jumped down off the steps and was heading around the side of the house.

"You've done this before—haven't you?" Evan demanded, following her.

"Maybe," she replied, grinning at him in the dark.

A loud howl somewhere nearby made them both stop.

"What was that?" Evan cried.

"A werewolf," Andy told him calmly. "Or maybe a cat."

They both laughed. Nervous laughter.

The back door was locked, too. But the kitchen window was open a crack. Evan pushed it open wider, and they crept into the dark kitchen.

Holding his breath, Evan could hear every sound. Their trainers scraped noisily against the linoleum. The refrigerator hummed. Water swirled in the dishwasher.

I can even hear the pounding of my heart, Evan thought. What am I doing? Have I really broken into Conan's house?

"This way," Andy whispered. "His room is probably upstairs."

Evan kept against the wall as he followed Andy to the front stairs. They passed the small living room, bathed in orange light. The floorboards creaked under their shoes. Evan stumbled over a pile of old newspapers stacked in the narrow hallway.

Up the wooden stairs. The banister squeaked under Evan's hand. A venetian blind rattled against an open window, startling him.

"Sure is dark," Andy muttered as they reached the top of the stairs.

Evan tried to reply, but his breath caught in his throat.

Holding on to the wall, he followed Andy to the first bedroom. She fumbled until she found a light switch, then clicked it on. The ceiling light revealed that they had found Conan's room.

They both stood in the doorway, waiting for their eyes to adjust to the light. Then they quickly glanced around.

The walls of the small, square room were filled with posters of sports stars. The biggest poster, above Conan's bed, showed Michael Jordan jumping about ten feet in the air as he slam-dunked a basketball. A bookshelf against one wall held very few books—but was loaded with sports trophies that Conan had won on various teams.

Suddenly, Andy started to laugh.

Evan turned to her, startled. "What's so funny?"

She pointed to Conan's bed. "Look—he still has a teddy bear!"

Evan turned his eyes to the bed, where a forlorn-looking, nearly flat, one-eyed teddy bear rested on the pillow. "Conan the Barbarian?" he cried, laughing. "He sleeps with a teddy bear?"

A loud creak made them cut their laughter short.

They listened hard, their eyes wide with fear. "Just the house," Evan whispered.

Andy shivered. "Enough fooling around. Let's find the Monster Blood and get out of here."

They moved into the centre of the room. "Where do you think he hid it?" Evan asked, pulling open the wardrobe door.

"He didn't," Andy replied.

"Huh?" Evan spun around.

Andy had the blue can of Monster Blood in her hand. Grinning, she held it up to show Evan.

Evan let out a surprised cry. "You found it? Where?"

"Right on this shelf," she replied, pointing. "He put it next to his tennis trophies."

Evan hurried over to her and took the blue can from her hand. As he held it up to examine it, the lid popped off.

The green Monster Blood began bubbling over the top of the can.

"It's growing fast!" Evan declared.

Andy stooped down and picked up the lid. She handed it to Evan. "Put it back on. Hurry."

Evan tried pushing the lid back on. It kept sliding off.

"Hurry up," Andy urged. "We've got to go."

"The Monster Blood—it's up over the top," Evan cried.

"Shove it down," Andy instructed.

Evan tried pushing the green gunk down into the can, pressing against it with the palm of his hand. Then he tried pushing it with three fingers.

He gasped as he felt the green goo tighten around his fingers and start to pull them down.

"It—it's got me!" Evan stammered.

Andy's mouth dropped open. "Huh?"

"It's got my fingers!" Evan cried shrilly. "It won't let go!"

As Andy hurried to help him, they both heard the front door slam.

"Someone's home!" Evan whispered, tugging to pull his fingers free. "We're caught!"

Andy froze in the centre of the room, her eyes wide with horror.

Evan nearly dropped the can of Monster Blood. The sticky green substance tightened its grip on his fingers, making loud sucking sounds.

But Evan only cared about the sounds coming from downstairs.

"I'm home!" he heard Conan shout.

"We're home, too!" It was a woman's voice, probably Conan's mother.

"They're all home," Evan whispered.

"We're dead meat!" Andy murmured.

"I'm going upstairs," Conan called to his parents.

Evan let out a terrified cry as he heard Conan's heavy footsteps on the stairs. "Andy— wh-what do we do?" he stammered.

"The window!" she replied.

They both lunged towards the open window and peered out. A narrow concrete ledge stretched just beneath the window.

Without hesitating, Andy raised a leg over the window-sill and climbed out on to the ledge. "Evan—hurry!" she whispered, gesturing frantically.

Evan was still desperately trying to pull his fingers from the bubbling green goo. Andy reached in through the window and grabbed him by the shoulder. "Evan—!"

He heard Conan's footsteps in the upstairs hall just outside the bedroom.

Using his free hand for support, Evan scrambled out of the window and joined Andy on the narrow ledge.

"D-don't look down," Andy instructed in a trembling whisper.

Evan didn't obey. He glanced down. The ground seemed very far below.

They each stood on a side of the window— Andy to the left, Evan the right. They pressed their bodies against the brick wall—and listened.

They heard Conan step into the room.

Did he notice that the light had been turned on?

No way to tell.

Loud rap music suddenly jarred the silence. Conan had turned on his boom box. He started chanting off-key along with the music.

Evan pressed as tightly against the side of the house as he could.

Go back downstairs, Conan, he pleaded silently. *Please—go back downstairs!*

How will Andy and I ever get away from here? he wondered, feeling all of his muscles tighten in panic.

Despite the hot night air, a cold chill ran down Evan's back. He shuddered so hard, he nearly toppled off the ledge.

The blue can stuck to his hand. The Monster Blood sucked at his fingers. But he couldn't worry about that now.

He could hear Conan moving around inside the room. Was he dancing to the loud music?

Evan glanced across the window at Andy. Her eyes were shut. Her face was clenched in a tight frown.

"Andy—!" Evan whispered. He knew that Conan couldn't hear a whisper over the booming music. "Andy—it'll be okay. As soon as he leaves, we'll jump inside and sneak down the stairs."

Andy nodded without opening her eyes. "Did I ever tell you I'm afraid of heights?" she whispered.

"No," Evan replied.

"Well, remind me to tell you!"

"We'll be okay," he murmured.

Clinging to the side of the house, Evan kept repeating those words to himself. "We'll be okay. We'll be okay. We'll be okay."

Then Trigger started to bark.

A low bark of surprise at first. And then a louder series of barks, insistent barks, excited barks.

Evan swallowed hard. He glanced down to the ground.

Trigger was peering at him, jumping against the side of the house, as if trying to reach the ledge. The dog barked louder with each jump.

"Trigger—no!" Evan called down in a frantic whisper.

That only made the dog bark more furiously.

Did Conan hear it? Could he hear Trigger's ferocious barks over the music?

"Trigger—stop! Go home! Go home!"

Suddenly the music stopped.

Trigger's excited barks rose up even louder against the new silence.

Conan *must* hear them now, Evan realized.

The cocker spaniel threw himself wildly against the side of the house, trying to get up to Evan and Andy. Despite Evan's frantic signals to be quiet, the stupid dog barked his head off.

Evan's breath caught in his throat as he heard Conan making his way to the window.

A second later, Conan stuck his head out. "What's going on?" he shouted.

Evan's knees buckled. He started to fall.

Evan clung to the brick wall and stopped his fall.

He stared at Conan's blond hair poking out of the window. Evan was close enough to reach out and touch it.

"Shut up down there!" Conan shouted.

That made Trigger bark even louder.

He's going to see us, Evan thought, trembling all over.

There's no way Conan won't see us.

"Conan—come downstairs!" Mrs Barber's voice floated up from downstairs. "Conan—come down and have your cake and ice cream. You said you were dying for dessert!" she called.

Conan's head disappeared back into the bedroom. "There's some stupid dog barking down there," he called to his mother.

Clinging to the side of the house, struggling to keep his quivering knees from buckling again, Evan shut his eyes and listened.

He heard Conan's footsteps cross the room. The bedroom light went out.

Silence.

"He—left," Evan choked out.

Andy let out a long breath. "I can't believe he didn't see us out here."

Evan glanced down to the ground. Trigger had finally stopped barking. But he continued to stand and stare up at them, his front paws against the side of the house, his stubby tail spinning like a propeller.

"Stupid dog," Evan muttered.

"Let's go," Andy urged. She didn't wait for Evan. She practically did a swan dive into the house.

It took Evan a few moments to get his legs to work. Then he ducked his head and climbed through the window after Andy.

Holding his breath, he led the way on tiptoe to the bedroom door. He stopped and listened.

Silence. No one on the dark landing.

He could hear the Barbers' voices downstairs in the kitchen.

He and Andy made their way to the top of the stairs. Then, holding tightly to the banister, they crept halfway down.

Evan stopped to listen again. Andy bumped right into him, nearly sending him sailing down the stairs. "Shhh!" she cried.

They could hear Conan talking to his parents

in the kitchen. He was complaining about the other guys on the basketball team. "They're all wimps," Evan heard Conan say.

"Well, that'll make you look even better," Mr Barber replied.

Evan took another deep breath and held it. Then he made his way down to the bottom of the stairs.

Almost out, he thought, his entire body shaking. Almost out of here.

He reached for the front doorknob.

"Conan, go upstairs and get your maths book," he heard Mr Barber say. "I want to see the homework you had trouble with."

"Okay," Conan replied. His chair scraped against the floor.

Andy grabbed Evan's shoulder.

They stared in frozen horror at each other— one foot away from escape—and waited to be caught.

"Conan—don't go now. Get the book later," Mrs Barber chimed in. Then they heard her scold Conan's father: "Let the boy have his cake and ice cream."

"Fine, fine," Mr Barber replied. "He can show me the book later."

Conan's chair scraped back into place under the table.

Evan didn't wait another second.

He jerked open the front door, pushed open the screen door, and burst out of the house like a rocket.

He could hear Andy gasping as she ran behind him. And then he could hear Trigger's shrill yips as the dog followed, too.

Down the Barbers' front lawn, into the street. Their trainers slapped the pavement as they ran full speed through the darkness.

They didn't stop until they reached Evan's drive.

Evan leaned against his family's mailbox and struggled to catch his breath. He raised his hand to wipe the sweat off his forehead—and saw the blue can still stuck there.

"Help me," he pleaded. He reached out his hand to Andy.

She was breathing hard, too. Her eyes kept darting back down the street, as if she expected Conan to be chasing after them.

"Close one," she murmured. She turned to Evan. Her eyes glowed excitedly in the light from the streetlamp. "That was fun!"

Evan didn't agree. In his opinion, it was far too scary to be fun. And here he was, still stuck to the can of Monster Blood.

He pushed his hand toward Andy. "Pull it off," he told her. "I think you need both hands. I can't do it."

She grabbed the can in both hands. The green gunk bubbled over the sides, making loud sucking sounds.

Andy tugged. Then tugged harder. Then she took a deep breath, leaned back, and tugged with all her might.

The Monster Blood finally let go of its grip on Evan's fingers. The can slid off with a loud *pop*. Andy went tumbling back on to the pavement.

"Ow!" Evan held up three fingers and tried to examine them under the streetlight. They were all wrinkled and pruney, the way they looked when he had been swimming for an hour or two.

"Yuck! That stuff is so gross!" he cried.

Andy climbed slowly to her feet. She still cradled the Monster Blood can in both hands. "At least we got it back," she murmured.

"Yeah. Now we can bury it again," Evan said, still examining his fingers.

"Huh? Bury it?" Andy pulled the can away, as if protecting it from Evan.

"You heard me," Evan said firmly. "It's just too dangerous to mess with, Andy. Take it home and bury it in your back yard, okay?"

Andy stared down at the can. She didn't reply.

"Bury it," Evan repeated. "Take it home and bury it. Promise?"

"Well . . ." Andy hesitated. Then she said, "Okay. Promise."

Evan woke up with a bad sore throat the next morning.

His mother worried that he might be coming down with the flu. So she kept him home from school. Evan spent the day reading comic books and watching MTV. His sore throat disappeared by mid-afternoon.

He returned to school the next day, feeling refreshed and ready to see everyone.

The good feeling lasted until he stepped into Mr Murphy's science class near the end of the day. Evan had to walk past the hamster cage to get to his seat.

As he neared the cage, he peered in.

That's weird, he thought. Where's Cuddles?

When did Mr Murphy get a rabbit?

A *rabbit*?

He stopped and leaned closer to the cage.

Familiar black eyes stared up at him. A familiar pink nose twitched at him.

It was Cuddles, Evan realized.

Cuddles had grown as big as a rabbit!

Evan leaned over the hamster cage, staring at the giant-sized Cuddles, as the bell rang. He turned to see that the other kids had all taken their seats.

"Evan, I see you're examining your victim," Mr Murphy said from the front of the room.

"I—uh—" Evan couldn't think of a reply. "Victim?"

Mr Murphy angrily narrowed his beady black eyes at Evan. "You've been overfeeding Cuddles, Evan. Look how fat he has become."

Almost as fat as you! Evan wanted to say.

Evan knew that Cuddles's weight problem wasn't his fault.

And it had nothing to do with overeating.

Cuddles had grown to triple-hamster size because of Monster Blood.

"When I find Andy, I'll *strangle* her!" Evan muttered.

"What did you say, Evan?" Mr Murphy demanded.

Evan could feel his face turning bright red. He hadn't meant to talk out loud.

"Uh . . . nothing," he replied, totally embarrassed. He slunk to his seat.

Andy has gone too far this time, he thought bitterly. She promised she'd bury the Monster Blood. She promised!

And now she's turned Cuddles into a fat freak! And Murphy thinks it's all my fault!

"Please stay after school," Mr Murphy told Evan, "so we can discuss Cuddles's diet."

Evan heard some kids snickering. He knew they were laughing at him.

He saw Conan and Biggie at their seats in the back. Conan was twitching his nose, puffing out his cheeks, pretending to be a fat hamster. Biggie was laughing his head off.

Evan stared at the hamster all through class. Cuddles appeared to grow right before Evan's eyes. With each breath, the hamster seemed to puff up wider and taller.

Its black eyes were as big as marbles now. They stared back at Evan, as if accusing him.

When the hamster moved to its water tube, the entire cage rattled and shook.

Please don't grow any more! Evan pleaded silently, staring at the shaking cage. *Please stop right now, Cuddles. Okay?*

The hamster breathed noisily. Wheezing gasps. Evan could hear Cuddles panting all the way across the room.

The cage shook again as Cuddles turned around. Evan watched in horror as the cage nearly toppled off its table.

I'll *kill* Andy! Evan thought bitterly. How could she *do* this to me?

When the bell rang, the other kids all gathered up their books and headed out of the room. Evan stood up and walked over to Cuddles's cage.

Panting loudly, Cuddles stared up at him. He's too big to fit on his wheel, Evan realized. If he grows any more, he'll burst out of the cage!

How much Monster Blood did Andy feed him? Evan wondered. He had to find out.

He turned to Mr Murphy, who was reading over some papers at his desk. "I've got to find someone," Evan called up to him. "I'll be right back."

"Don't take too long," the teacher replied without looking up.

Evan hurried from the room—and ran into Conan. "Hey, I was looking for you," Conan said, sidestepping to the right, then the left, and stretching out both arms to keep Evan from getting away.

"No time now," Evan said sharply. But Conan wouldn't let him pass. "I'm kind of in a hurry,"

Evan told him. "I don't have time to be stuffed into my locker right now."

A big grin crossed Conan's handsome face. "Hey, I'm sorry about that," he said, his blue eyes twinkling.

"Huh? You're sorry?" Evan's mouth dropped open in shock.

"Yeah. No hard feelings," Conan said, lowering his eyes. "Shake."

Evan stuck out his hand. Then remembered Conan's crushing handshake. He tried to pull back his hand.

Too late.

Conan gripped it tightly and began to squeeze. As he squeezed Evan's hand, his grin grew wider and wider.

Down the hall, Evan saw Andy heading out of the door. He tried to call to her. But all that came out of his mouth was a squeak of pain.

Andy disappeared out of the front door of the school.

The bones in Evan's hand cracked and crunched.

When Conan finally let go, the hand looked like a sad lump of soft red clay.

"Wow! That's some handshake you've got!" Conan cried, laughing. He pretended his hand hurt. He shook it hard and blew on it. "You killed me that time! Have you been working out or something?"

Conan headed off to basketball practice, laughing and shaking his hand.

He really cracks himself up, Evan thought. An angry cry burst from his throat. He slammed his good hand into a locker. He was so furious, he thought he could feel steam pouring out of his ears.

"Evan—you're keeping me waiting!" Mr Murphy called in a singsong from the classroom doorway.

"Coming," Evan muttered miserably, and slunk back into the room.

He tried calling Andy for hours that night. But there was no one at home.

In his sleep, he dreamed that Trigger ate a big glob of Monster Blood and grew to giant size. Evan tried to stop him. But the enormous dog took off after the postman.

It wasn't much of a chase. Trigger caught the postman easily. The postman was the size of a hamster.

Evan woke up drenched with sweat. He glanced at his bedside clock. Only six in the morning. He normally didn't get up until seven.

He climbed out of bed anyway, feeling shaky and scared.

He decided he had to get to school before everyone else. He *had* to see if Cuddles had grown any bigger.

"Evan—where are you going?" his mother called sleepily as Evan headed out of the front door.

"Uh—school," Evan replied. He had hoped to sneak out before she woke up.

"So early?" She padded into the room, struggling with the belt to her blue cotton dressing-gown.

"Well . . . I have a science project I need to work on," Evan told her. It was *almost* the truth.

"A science project?" She eyed him suspiciously.

"Yeah. It's . . . big!" Evan replied, thinking quickly. "It's really big! So I couldn't bring it home."

"You're going without any breakfast?" Mrs Ross demanded, yawning.

"I'll grab something at school," he said. "See you later, Mum." He disappeared through the door before she could ask any more questions.

A red sun was just climbing over the trees in a grey sky. The air still carried the chill of the night. The lawns Evan passed shimmered wetly with morning dew.

He jogged the whole way, his backpack flopping heavily on his shoulder. There were no other kids in the playground or on the path heading into the building.

He crept into the school and made his way

down the silent, empty hall. His trainers echoed loudly as he trotted towards the science class-room.

Maybe Cuddles didn't grow overnight, Evan told himself.

Maybe he didn't grow at all. Maybe he shrank. Maybe he shrank back to his old size.

It was possible.

It was possible that Andy had fed the hamster only a teeny tiny speck of Monster Blood. Just enough for Cuddles to swell up to the size of a fat rabbit—then shrink right back down to cute, cuddly hamster size.

It *was* possible—wasn't it?

Yes! Yes! Evan crossed his fingers on both hands. He wished he could cross his toes.

By the time he reached the classroom, he was breathless. His heart thudded loudly in his chest.

He hesitated at the door.

Please, Cuddles—be small. Be small!

Then Evan took a deep breath, held it—and stepped inside.

Evan stepped into the room, staring at the cage against the far wall. At first, he didn't see Cuddles.

Had Cuddles shrunk? Had he?

Sometimes prayers are answered, Evan told himself. Sometimes good things happen.

Evan took a few hesitant steps closer. Then a few more steps.

Every muscle in his body had tensed. He was so frightened, it was actually hard to walk.

He could feel the blood throbbing at his temples. He mopped the cold beads of sweat off his forehead.

He still couldn't see Cuddles. Where was he? Where?

Grey morning light filtered in through the windows. The floor creaked under Evan's trainers.

Evan took another hesitant step towards the cage.

Another step.

Then he cried out in horror.

Evan hadn't seen Cuddles at first—because Cuddles was too *big*!

Cuddles filled the entire cage.

Evan held back, gaping in disbelief.

The hamster groaned noisily with every loud breath. It let out several disgusting grunts as its body pressed against the wire cage.

Its big, furry head pushed up against the top of the cage. Evan could see one enormous black eye, the size of a jar lid, staring out at him.

"No!" Evan cried out loud, feeling his knees begin to tremble. "This is impossible!"

The hamster uttered a few more low grunts.

The cage shook on its table.

The big black eye glared out at Evan.

And then as Evan stared in horrified disbelief, the hamster reached up its two pink paws. The toes slipped around the wires of the cage.

Cuddles let out an ugly groan.

Evan saw Cuddles's spongy pink nose twitch. He saw a flash of big white teeth.

Another groan.

The two front paws pushed against the cage wires.

The wires bent away.

Cuddles grunted again, wheezing loudly, excitedly.

He pushed the cage wires apart.

Then he started to squeeze his big, fur-covered body through the opening.

What do I do? Evan frantically asked himself.

What do I do now?

Cuddles is escaping!

"So what did you do?" Andy asked.

They were sitting together in the tall grass of the tiny park, watching the brown creek trickle past. The late afternoon sun felt warm on their backs. Crickets chirped in the trees behind them.

Three boys rolled past on bikes on the other side of the creek, heading home from school. One of them waved to Evan. He didn't wave back.

Andy wore a bright red sleeveless T-shirt over white denim jeans. She had slipped off her yellow trainers and was digging her bare feet into the soft ground.

"So what did you do?" she repeated.

Evan picked up a hard clump of dirt and tossed it into the creek. Then he leaned back, his hands planted firmly behind him on the ground.

"I got a dog lead," he told Andy. "From the supply cupboard."

94

Andy's eyes widened in surprise. "Murphy keeps a dog lead? What for?"

Evan shrugged. "He has all kinds of junk in there."

"So you put the lead on Cuddles?"

"Yeah," Evan told her. "He was just the right size. As big as a dog. Maybe a little bigger."

"As big as Trigger?" Andy demanded.

Evan nodded. "Then I tied the other end to the leg of Murphy's desk—and I ran out of there as fast as I could."

Andy laughed. But she cut it short when she caught Evan's angry glare. "What happened when you went to science class?" she asked, turning back to the creek.

"I didn't," Evan muttered.

"Huh?"

"I didn't go," Evan said softly. "I was afraid to go. I didn't want Murphy to start blaming me in front of everyone."

"So you cut class?" Andy asked, startled.

Evan nodded.

"So what did you do?" Andy asked. She pulled up a handful of the tall grass and let it sift through her fingers.

"I sneaked out and came here," Evan replied, frowning.

"Everyone was talking about Cuddles all day," Andy reported. Her dark eyes flashed. She couldn't keep an amused grin off her face.

"Everyone had to go in and see him. The stupid hamster practically caused a riot!"

"It isn't funny," Evan murmured.

"It's *kind* of funny!" Andy insisted. "Mr Murphy was bragging that Cuddles could beat up any other hamster in the country. He said he was going to try to get Cuddles on TV!"

"Huh?" Evan jumped to his feet. "You mean Mr Murphy wasn't upset?"

"I heard that he was at first," Andy replied thoughtfully. "But then I guess he got used to Cuddles being so big. And he was acting rather proud. You know. Like he had the biggest pumpkin at the fair or something. A blue-ribbon winner!" Andy snickered.

Evan kicked at the grass. "I know he's going to blame me. I know it!"

"Everyone was feeding Cuddles carrots all day," Andy said, not seeming to hear Evan's unhappy wails. "The hamster ate the carrots whole. One big chomp. Then it made this really disgusting swallowing sound. It was a riot."

"I can't believe this!" Evan groaned. He lowered his eyes angrily to Andy. "Why did you do it? Why?"

Andy gazed up at him innocently. "I wanted to give you a laugh," she replied.

"Huh? A laugh?" he shrieked.

"You were looking pretty down. I thought it might cheer you up."

Evan let out an angry cry.

"I suppose it didn't cheer you up," Andy muttered. She pulled up another handful of grass and let the blades fall over the legs of her white jeans.

Evan stomped over to the edge of the stream. He kicked a rock into the water.

"Come on, Evan," Andy called. "You have to admit it's a *little* funny."

He spun around to face her. "It's not," he insisted. "Not funny at all. What if Cuddles just keeps growing and growing? Then what?"

"We could put a saddle on his back and give everyone hamster rides!" She giggled.

Evan scowled and kicked another rock into the creek. "You *know* how dangerous that Monster Blood is," he scolded. "What are we going to do? How are we going to get Cuddles back to hamster size?"

Andy shrugged. She pulled up another handful of grass.

The sun sank lower behind the trees. A shadow rolled over them. Two little kids chased a white-and-red soccer ball on the other side of the stream. Their mother shouted to them not to get wet.

"Where's the Monster Blood can?" Evan demanded, standing over Andy. "Maybe it tells the antidote on the can. Maybe it tells how to reverse the whole thing."

97

Andy shook her head. "Evan, you know it doesn't say anything on the can. No instructions. No ingredients. Nothing." She climbed to her feet and brushed off the legs of her jeans. "I've got to get home. My aunt doesn't know where I am. She's probably having a cow."

Evan followed her towards the street, shaking his head. "How big?" he muttered.

She glanced back at him. "What did you say?"

"How big will Cuddles be tomorrow?" Evan asked in a trembling voice. "How big?"

"Andy—will you hurry up?"

Evan had agreed to meet Andy at her aunt's house the next morning so they could go to school early. But Andy had found a spot on her jeans and had gone back up to her room to change.

And now they were no longer early.

"Sorry," she said, hurtling down the stairs two steps at a time. She had changed her entire outfit. Now she had on a red-and-black-striped vest over a yellow T-shirt, pulled down over pale blue shorts.

"Didn't you leave out a colour?" Evan demanded sarcastically, grabbing Andy's backpack for her and hurrying to the front door.

She made a face at him. "I like bright colours. It suits my personality."

"Your personality is *late*!" he declared.

She followed him out of the door and down the front path to the pavement. "At least I *have* a personality!" she cried. "What's the rush, anyway?"

Evan didn't answer. He adjusted his backpack on his shoulder, then began running towards school.

"Hey—wait for me!" Andy called, running after him.

"How much Monster Blood did you give Cuddles, anyway?" Evan demanded without slowing his pace. "The whole can?"

"No way!" Andy called breathlessly. "Just a spoonful. He seemed to like it."

"I expect he liked being as big as a dog, too," Evan said, turning the corner. The tall, redbrick school building came into view.

"Maybe he's back to normal today," Andy said.

But as they came near the building, it was easy to tell that things were *not* normal.

Evan heard a loud crash from the side of the building. It sounded like glass shattering.

Then he heard excited shouts. Loud kids' voices filled with alarm.

"What's going *on*?" Andy cried.

"They dived up the stairs and burst into the building. Running at full speed, they turned the corner and made their way to the science classroom.

Evan reached it a few steps ahead of Andy. Hearing excited shouts and cries, he lurched into the room—and then stopped with a startled cry.

"No! Oh please—no!"

"Stand back! Everyone stand back!" a red-faced Mr Murphy was screaming.

Cuddles uttered a loud grunt and flailed his giant legs wildly in the air.

"He—he's ten feet tall!" Evan heard Andy scream at his side.

"Al-almost!" Evan stammered.

The grunting, groaning hamster towered over Mr Murphy. Its pink paws batted the air. Its monstrous mouth opened wide, revealing two enormous, sharp white teeth.

"Back! Everyone back!" Mr Murphy shrieked.

The terrified kids in the classroom pressed back against the walls.

Mr Murphy picked up a wooden chair in one hand, the torn dog lead in the other. Holding the chair by the back, he came at the grunting monster like a lion tamer.

"Down, Cuddles! Get down! Sit! Sit!"

He poked the wooden chair up at the giant hamster and snapped the dog lead like a whip.

Cuddles's watery black eyes, as big as soccer balls, glared down at the red-faced teacher. The hamster didn't seem terribly impressed with Mr Murphy's lion-tamer act.

"Down, Cuddles! Get down!" The teacher's chins quivered, and his big belly bounced up and down beneath his tight grey polo shirt.

Cuddles pulled back his huge lips and bared his white teeth. He let out a growl that made the light fixtures shake.

Terrified cries rang out through the room. Evan glanced back to see a horrified crowd of teachers and students jammed in the doorway.

"Down, Cuddles!"

Mr Murphy shoved the wooden chair up at the raging hamster. He cracked the dog lead whip near the hamster's throbbing, fur-covered belly.

The huge black eyes stared down angrily at Mr Murphy. The pink hamster paws clawed in the air.

Andy grabbed Evan's shoulder and held on tight. "This is terrible!" she cried. "Terrible!"

Evan started to reply—but frightened shrieks drowned out his words.

Cuddles grabbed the chair with both paws.

"Drop! Drop!" Mr Murphy screamed. He struggled to hold on to the chair.

Cuddles pulled the chair. Mr Murphy desperately held tight. He let the lead fall so he could hold on to the chair with both hands.

The teacher and Cuddles had a short tug-of-war.

Cuddles won easily. The hamster pulled the chair up, nearly jerking Mr Murphy's arms out of their sockets.

With a loud groan, the teacher toppled heavily to the floor.

Kids screamed.

Two teachers rushed forward to help the gasping Mr Murphy to his feet.

Evan stared up as the hamster raised the wooden chair to its mouth. The enormous white teeth opened quickly. The pink nose twitched. The watery black eyes blinked.

Then Cuddles chewed the wooden chair to pieces.

Splinters rained down on the floor.

The chomping teeth sounded like a lumberjack's axe biting into a tree.

Evan froze in horror along with everyone else in the room.

Andy was squeezing his shoulder so hard it hurt. "This is *our* fault," she murmured.

"*Our* fault?" Evan cried. "*Our* fault?"

She ignored his sarcasm. He saw the fear in her eyes as she stared up at the hamster. Cuddles had turned the chair into toothpicks!

"We've got to do something, Evan," she whispered, huddled close to him.

"But what?" Evan replied in a trembling voice. "What can we do?"

Then, suddenly, he had an idea.

"Come with me!" Evan cried, tugging Andy's arm.

She hesitated, staring up at the giant hamster. "Where?"

"I have an idea," Evan told her. "But we have to hurry!"

Cuddles lumbered over to Mr Murphy's desk. The hamster's heavy footsteps made the floor sag.

"Here, fella! Here!" Mr Murphy was tossing handfuls of sunflower seeds up to Cuddles. Cuddles glared down at him. The seeds were too small to bother with.

"Hurry!" Evan pleaded. He pulled Andy through the frightened crowd of kids and teachers at the door. Then he began running at full speed towards the auditorium.

"We can't just run away! We have to *do* something!" Andy cried.

"We're not running away," Evan called back

to her, turning a corner. "My father's sculpture—it's in the auditorium."

"Huh?" Andy's eyes narrowed in confusion. "Evan—have you totally *lost* it? Why do you want to look at your father's sculpture now?"

He burst through the auditorium doors and ran past the dark rows of seats toward the stage. Several pieces of sculpture had been set up there.

"Evan—I don't get it!" Andy cried, right behind him.

"Look," Evan said breathlessly. He pointed to his father's work near the back of the stage. "My dad's sculpture. It's just like a hamster wheel—see?"

Her mouth dropped open as she stared at it.

"It's a big metal wheel and it spins," Evan explained as they pulled themselves up on to the stage. "Come on. Help me drag it back to Murphy's room. It's big enough for Cuddles."

"Whoa!" Andy cried. "You want to bring Cuddles a wheel? What for?"

"To distract him," Evan replied, grabbing one side of the big sculpture. "If we can get Cuddles running on this wheel, it will give us time to work out where to keep him. And it will stop him from chewing the whole school to pieces."

Andy grabbed hold of the other side, one hand on the wheel, one hand on the platform. "Maybe Cuddles will run so hard, he'll lose weight.

Maybe he'll shrink back to his normal size," she said.

Luckily, the platform was on wheels. They rolled the sculpture towards the stage door at the side. "I just want to distract him," Evan said, tugging hard. "I just want to give us time to think, to make a plan."

"Wow! This is heavy!" Andy cried. They rolled it into the hall. "Heavy enough for Cuddles, I guess."

"I hope," Evan replied solemnly.

By the time they rolled the sculpture to the classroom, the crowd of frightened kids and teachers had grown even bigger. "Make way! Make way!" they both shouted, pushing their way through the crowd.

They set the wheel down in the centre of the floor and gazed over at Cuddles. The hamster had two teachers cornered, their backs pressed against the blackboard. It was gnashing its huge teeth at them, slapping its pink paws together as if eager to fight them.

Evan gasped when he saw Mr Murphy's desk, crushed flat on the floor.

"I—I've called the police!" Mr Murphy cried, his face beaded with large drops of sweat. "I begged them to come. But when I said it was a giant hamster, they didn't believe me! They thought it was a practical joke!"

"Stand back, everyone!" Evan cried shrilly.

"Stand back—please! Let Cuddles see the wheel!"

The giant hamster turned suddenly. The two teachers scrambled away from the wall. Kids and teachers screamed and hurried towards the door.

"Maybe he'll run on the wheel for a while," Andy explained to Mr Murphy. "Then we can figure out what to do with him!"

"He—he sees it!" Mr Murphy cried breathlessly, all of his chins quivering at once.

Cuddles stared down at the wheel. His stub of a tail thudded loudly against the blackboard. He dropped heavily to all fours and took a lumbering step towards the wheel.

"He sees it. He's going to it," Evan murmured softly.

A hush fell over the room as everyone stared at the hamster.

Will Cuddles climb inside? Evan wondered, holding his breath.

Will he run on the wheel?

Will my plan work?

The hamster sniffed the wheel. Its pink nose twitched. It uttered a low grunt.

Then it raised itself back on to his hind legs. The hamster's massive shadow fell over the room.

With another disgusting grunt, it picked the sculpture up in its front paws and raised it to its face.

"No!" Evan cried. "Cuddles—no!"

The metal clanged as Cuddles bit into the wheel. Evan saw deep tooth marks in the aluminium. Cuddles bit down again. Then, seeing that he couldn't chew the wheel up, he pulled it apart, holding the sculpture in his paws and twisting it furiously with his teeth.

Then he tossed the mangled wheel away. It slammed into a window, shattering it into a thousand pieces.

"Back to the drawing board," Andy muttered to Evan.

Evan shook his head glumly. That plan was useless, he told himself. Now what?

He didn't have time to think about it.

He heard shrill cries and shrieks of terror.

"Put him down! Cuddles—put him down!" Mr Murphy was screaming.

Evan turned and saw that the giant hamster had picked up a kid.

Conan!

Cuddles held Conan in both paws and was raising him toward his gaping mouth.

"Drop! Drop!" Mr Murphy was shouting.

Conan thrashed his arms and legs. "Help me! Ohhh, helllp me!" he shrieked. He started to cry. Gasping sobs. Tears rolled down his red cheeks.

"Helllp! Mummmmm! Mummmmmmm! Helllp me!"

Normally Evan would have enjoyed watching Conan cry like a baby. But this was too serious. Cuddles could chew Conan in half! Evan realized.

He grabbed Andy. "Where's the Monster Blood?"

"Huh? In my locker. I hid it under a bunch of stuff in my locker. Why?"

"I need it," Evan said. "Come on. I have another idea."

"I hope it's better than the last one," Andy muttered.

They hurried to the door, then glanced back.

Cuddles was playing with Conan, tossing him from paw to paw, licking him with his huge, pink tongue. Conan was wailing his head off.

Evan led the way to Andy's locker. "I'm going to eat some Monster Blood," he told her, thinking out loud. "I'll eat a lot. I'll grow bigger than Cuddles."

"I get it," Andy said, running beside him. "You'll turn yourself into a giant. You'll make yourself as big as Cuddles."

"No," Evan replied. "Bigger. Much bigger. I'll make myself so big that Cuddles will look hamster size. Then I'll stuff him in the supply cupboard and lock the door."

"It's a stupid plan," Andy said.

"I know," Evan agreed.

"But it's worth a try," Andy added.

Evan swallowed hard and didn't reply. He was staring across the hall at Andy's locker.

"Oh, no!" Andy cried out when she saw what Evan was gaping at.

The locker door bulged as if about to burst open. And green goo poured out from the sides and the bottom.

"The Monster Blood—it outgrew my locker!" Andy cried.

Evan ran up to it and grabbed the door handle. He started to tug. "Is it locked?"

"No," Andy replied, hanging back.

Evan tugged. He tugged harder. With a loud

groan, he tugged with both hands. "It won't open!" he cried.

"Let me try it," Andy said.

But before she could step forward, the locker door burst open with a loud *whoooosh*.

Sticky, green gunk splashed over Evan.

He didn't have a chance to cry out.

It poured over him like a tall, cresting ocean wave.

An ocean wave of Monster Blood.

It's *burying* me! Evan realized.

The huge, sticky glob splashed out of the locker, plopped over him, smothering him, choking him.

It's sucking me in! I can't move!

I can't move!

Evan shut his eyes as the heavy, green gunk rolled over his head. He shot his arms out, trying to push it away.

As it swept over him, he fell to his knees. Kicking and thrashing, it forced him down to the floor.

I'm stuck inside, he thought. Stuck inside . . .

He felt hands grab his ankles.

The hands tugged hard.

He began to slide. Over the floor. Over the thick layer of Monster Blood.

"I've got you!" he heard Andy cry. "I've got you out!"

He opened his eyes. He saw her pulling him, tugging him out of the thick green gunk by the ankles.

It clung to his clothes and his skin. But he was out.

"Thanks," he murmured weakly. He climbed shakily to his feet.

He could hear Conan screaming and crying back in the classroom. There was still time to save him, Evan realized.

He pulled a hunk of Monster Blood off the quivering green mound—and jammed it into his mouth.

"I'm going to be sick," Andy groaned, holding her stomach.

Evan swallowed and reached for another mouthful. "It doesn't taste bad," he told her. "A little lemony."

"Don't eat too much!" she cried, half-covering her eyes as she watched him swallow another mouthful.

"I have to grow big enough so that Cuddles is hamster size compared to me," Evan said. He grabbed another hunk.

He could already feel himself start to grow. His head was already over the tops of the lockers.

Back in the classroom, Conan let out another terrified wail.

"Let's go!" Evan boomed. His voice thundered deeply in his new, larger body. He could feel himself growing taller. Taller.

He had to lower his head to get through the classroom door.

Kids and teachers moved out of his way, crying out their surprise and alarm.

He crossed the room, passed Mr Murphy, and

113

stepped up to the giant hamster. "I'm as big as Cuddles!" Evan called down to Andy.

He reached out and lifted Conan from Cuddles's paws. Cuddles reached out to take Conan back. But Evan lowered him gently to the floor.

"Hellllp me! Helllp me!" Conan ran bawling from the room.

Evan turned to face the hamster. They stared at each other eye to eye.

Cuddles's huge pink nose twitched. He sniffed Evan, inhaling so hard that Evan was nearly sucked forward.

Evan took a step back.

Keep growing! he urged himself. *I've got to keep growing!*

Cuddles eyed him warily, still sniffing. His watery black eyes stared hard as if trying to figure out if Evan was friend or foe.

"Don't you remember me, Cuddles?" Evan said softly. "Remember, I'm the one who fed you after school every day?"

Keep growing! he silently urged himself.

Why aren't I growing any taller?

Down below, he could see Andy, Mr Murphy and the others huddled against the far wall, staring up at the two giants in hushed terror.

Keep growing! Keep growing!

There was no way he could pick Cuddles up now, Evan realized. They were exactly the same

114

height. And Cuddles outweighed him by at least a ton!

Keep growing!

"What's wrong, Andy?" Evan called down to her in a trembling voice. "I ate tons of the stuff. Why did I stop growing?"

"I don't know!" she called up to him. Her voice sounded as tiny as a mouse's squeak.

He saw that she had the blue can in her hand. She was turning it over, reading the label. "I don't know, Evan!" she shouted. "I don't know why you're not growing!"

Then, as Evan turned back to face Cuddles, the hamster reached out and grabbed his waist with both front paws.

"Ow!" Evan cried as the hamster tried to lift him off the floor.

Gazing up, he saw the gaping hamster mouth open, the sharp white teeth emerge.

Evan squirmed desperately, pulling himself loose. Then he wrapped both arms around the hamster's middle.

They started to wrestle. Evan fought hard, but the hamster overpowered him. Cuddles rolled Evan on to his back on the floor.

The two giants wrestled over the floor, surrounded by the shrill screams of teachers and kids.

Grow bigger! Grow bigger—now! Evan pleaded.

115

But it was too late, he saw.

The hamster lowered its hot, furry body over him. Evan could feel the creature's booming heartbeat as it pressed him to the floor.

Then its teeth rose up over Evan's head.

The hamster's mouth opened wide.

The teeth swung down.

A wave of hot, sour hamster breath blew down over Evan.

He shut his eyes.

"Sorry," he murmured to Andy.

He held his breath and waited for the teeth to clamp down.

Evan heard a *pop*, like the sound of a cork flying off a bottle.

Still sprawled on his back on the floor, Evan opened his eyes.

"Huh?" Cuddles had disappeared. Vanished.

Evan stared up at the startled faces of kids and teachers against the wall. "Wh-where's Cuddles?" he stammered.

Andy stood frozen like a statue, her mouth open.

Evan slowly realized that she was nearly as big as he was. In fact, *everyone* was about his size.

He pulled himself up to a sitting position. "Hey—I'm back to a normal size!" he cried. He shook his head hard as if trying to shake away his close call with the giant hamster.

"There's Cuddles!" Andy cried, pointing.

Evan turned to see Cuddles huddled against the wall. "He's a little hamster again!" Evan exclaimed happily. He took three quick steps, bent down, and grabbed Cuddles between his hands. "Gotcha!"

Holding the hamster in front of him, he turned back to Andy and the others. "What happened? Why did we shrink back?"

Andy was studying the blue Monster Blood can. Suddenly she tossed back her dark hair, her brown eyes lit up, and she started to laugh. "It's the expiry date!" she cried happily. "The expiry date on the can—it's *today*! The Monster Blood stops working today! The magic has worn out!"

Evan let out a whoop of joy.

Mr Murphy, a wide grin on his round face, hurried over and put his arm around Evan's shoulders. "Fine job, Evan! Fine job!" he exclaimed. "You saved the school. I'm proud of you!"

"Thanks, Mr Murphy," Evan replied, awkwardly.

"You'll never make a basketball player now that you're short again," Mr Murphy said, smiling. "But that was quite a good match with Cuddles. Have you ever thought of trying out for the wrestling team?"

Andy came to Evan's house for dinner that night. He greeted her at the door, eager to tell her how all the kids had apologized for not believing him about the Monster Blood.

But before he could say anything, she held up a large brown envelope and grinned at him.

"What's that?" he asked, following her into the living room.

"It's a present my parents sent me from Europe," she replied, her grin growing wider. "You won't *believe* what it is."

She started to pull open the envelope. But the front doorbell rang.

Evan hurried to see who it was.

"Mr Murphy!" he cried in surprise.

"Hi, Evan," the teacher said, his round body nearly filling the entire doorway. "Hope I'm not interrupting your dinner."

"No," Evan replied. "Want to come in?"

"No thanks," Mr Murphy replied. His expression turned solemn. "I came by because I thought you should have some sort of reward, Evan. You were a real hero at school today."

"Aw, not really," Evan said awkwardly. He could feel his face growing hot and knew he was blushing.

What kind of reward? Evan wondered, staring back at the teacher. A cash reward?

Mr Murphy raised the hamster cage into Evan's view. "I've decided to reward you with Cuddles," the teacher said. "I know how fond of him you are."

"No, please!" Evan started to plead.

"It's a small token," Mr Murphy said. "To show how grateful I am. How grateful we all are."

"Please—no—!"

But before Evan realized it, the hamster cage was in his hand, and Mr Murphy was waddling back down the drive to his car.

"He gave you Cuddles?" Andy asked as Evan returned to the living room carrying the cage. He set it down on the coffee table.

"It's my reward," Evan told her, rolling his eyes. "Do you believe it?"

"Well, you *won't* believe this!" Andy declared. "Look what my parents found in Europe!"

She reached into the envelope and pulled out a blue plastic can. "It's Monster Blood!"

"Oh, no!" Evan wailed.

"They wrote that they remembered how much fun I had with the old can," Andy said, holding up the blue container. "So when they saw this can in a toy shop in Germany, they decided to send me a new one."

Evan's eyes went wide with fear. "You— you're not going to open it?" he demanded warily.

"Already did," Andy replied. "Just to take a look. But I'm not going to use it. Really. I promise."

Evan started to say something—but he was interrupted by his mother's call from the kitchen. "Dinnertime, you two! Wash your hands and come to the table!"

Andy put the can of Monster Blood down on the desk in the corner. They obediently hurried to wash their hands.

They had a lively dinner. There was *lots* to talk about. They laughed and joked about all that had happened at school. It was easy to laugh about it now that it was all over.

After dinner, Evan and Andy returned to the living room.

Andy was the first to see that the door to the hamster cage was wide open. The cage was empty.

Evan was the one who spotted Cuddles on the desk.

"Cuddles—what are you eating?" he cried. "What are you eating?"

The
Babysitters
Club

Need a babysitter? Then call the Babysitters Club. Kristy Thomas and her friends are all experienced sitters. They can tackle any job from rampaging toddlers to a pandemonium of pets. To find out all about them, read on!

Hippo Fantasy

Lose yourself in a whole new world, a world where anything is possible – from wizards and dragons, to time travel and new civilizations . . . Gripping, thrilling, scary and funny by turns, these Hippo Fantasy titles will hold you captivated to the very last page.

The Night of Wishes
Michael Ende (author of *The Neverending Story*)

It's New Year's Eve, and Beelzebub Preposteror, sorceror and evil-doer, has only seven hours to complete his annual share of villainous deeds and *completely destroy the world!*

Rowan of Rin
Emily Rodda

The witch Sheba has made a mysterious prophecy, which is like a riddle. A riddle Rowan must solve if he is to find out the secret of the mountain and save Rin from disaster . . .

The Wednesday Wizard
Sherryl Jordan

Denzil, humble apprentice to the wizard Valvasor, is in a real pickle. When he tries to reach his master to warn him of a dragon attack, he mucks up the spell and ends up seven centuries into the future!

The Practical Princess
Jay Williams

The Practical Princess has the gift of common sense. And when you spend your days tackling dragons and avoiding marriage to unsuitable suitors, common sense definitely comes in useful!